Praise for Baba Yaga and the Stepmother

Rypma's lyrical prose transports the reader into a world of magic steeped in history and folklore.

Her compelling heroine navigates palace intrigue and cryptic prophecy on the way to her paradigm shifting happily-ever-after.

— Kate Koppy
Author of *Fairy Tales in
Contemporary American Culture*

An inspired recasting of "Snow White and the Seven Dwarfs"— not the Disney film but the much earlier version recounted by the Brothers Grimm, itself based on a long-maintained oral tradition. In this case the story is told from the stepmother's point of view, while other liberties thematically update and enliven the proceedings.

Tatania (aka Tanya) is a self-reliant, feminist heroine, a take-charge kind of country girl well-prepared for her journey to the big city (Moscow, aka Moskva). Under protection of a shape-shifting forest witch, she takes on the role of stepmother to the unsympathetic Snow White character (aka Snowdrop) when the widowed heir to Russia's throne chooses her as his second wife.

The narrative unfolds in richly surprising detail, not unlike the nesting matryoshka dolls that constitute a key image herein.

—Tom Patterson
Author of *St. EOM in the Land of Pasaquan
Howard Finster, Stranger from Another World
The Tom Patterson Years*

Other Books By Judith Rypma

Fiction:

In the Shadows With Catherine the Great (Book One)

Mrs. Fleeney's Flowers

The Amber Beads

Poetry:

Worshipping at Lenin's Mausoleum

Amber Notes

Sewing Lessons

Forget-Me-Not

Looking for the Amber Room

Rocks In My Head: Poetry for Young People About Rocks, Minerals, and Crystals

Mineral Treasures

Rapunzel's Hair

Holy Rocks

Baba Yaga
And The Stepmother

A Retelling of Snow White

JUDITH A. RYPMA

ISBN: 978-1-7367311-5-4 (Paperback)

Cover Design by Shelley Savoy

Author photo by Beth Koster

Orange Abalone Press

Interior design by Booknook.biz

For Sue McMillin:

No words of thanks could ever suffice.
A true lifetime friendship is a dream come true.

On Fairytales, especially for adults

"Every person's life is a fairytale written by God's fingers."

— Han Christian Andersen

Table of Contents

Baba Yaga And The Stepmother

A Retelling of Snow White

Chapter 1

A witch inhabited the forest.

"Not always, only at certain times," Lady Tatiana's beloved mother had warned before her death many years ago.

"What does she look like?" Tatiana had asked.

"She has a sharp forehead and a protruding chin and nose."

"What else?" Tatiana demanded, though admittedly she was more fascinated by bunnies hopping in and out of their nest in the meadow where she and her mother gathered herbs.

"She is all bones. Even her hut is fashioned from bones and blood."

"Where is her hut?"

Her mother shrugged and then lowered her voice: "It is everywhere and nowhere."

"What does that mean?"

"It means you should expect her at any time and any place and always treat her kindly. That way she might do the same for you."

This made little sense. On the countless occasions she'd wandered the forest in subsequent years and now as a young woman, Tatiana had seen nothing witch-like. Only in the stories that her mother told her and had started writing down before her death did the witch seem real.

The forest served as Tatiana's retreat from an otherwise dull life in a small castle beside a sleepy village spreading outward from its moat. She lived in Tolkov Castle with her widowed father and a handful of servants. As often as she could, she sought the solace of silver leaves that quivered in tune with the wind and the towering pines, spruces, and firs pointing their palette of greens toward the faraway Ural Mountains.

By now she had an unerring sense of other woodland landmarks: gooseberry and blackberry bushes, hollow logs sought by small animals and honeybees, mushroom shelves, vines entwined up deciduous tree trunks, and the dens where brown and black bears retreated each winter. The bears did not frighten her the way a witch might have, no more than did the raccoons, deer, hedgehogs, rabbits, raccoons, grouse, and other forest creatures with whom she often became friends.

Her mother had taught her how to identify various herbs and wildflowers sprinkling the forest floor and occasional meadows. From her Tatiana had learned to recognize most leaves, types of tree bark, butterfly species, and bird calls. Later, her father had introduced his young daughter to the habits and habitats of various animals. Almost from the time she could walk, he taught her how to wield a bow and arrow to procure just enough furs and meat upon which to subsist in difficult times, and not a morsel more.

Today she'd set her sights on a trio of squirrels scampering around a giant oak. She tried not to laugh at their endless chatter and playful antics, so much so that her bow arm started to shake. She knew one of the squirrels could be sacrificed now that summer waned and food would soon be in short supply. Still, she couldn't do it. She would leave it to the estate's huntsmen.

Taking a seat on a fallen maple trunk, she blew seeds from silky milkweed strands bursting from their pods. The cottony material she slipped into her pouch to bring half to the village healer for bandages and the other half to the local apothecary.

Behind her the squirrels quieted, as did the wind that a short time ago had blown her waist-length reddish-gold hair around her ears and into her eyes. The usual late afternoon squawks of blue jays and crows ceased.

She peered through the tree trunks, where a faint rose tinge from the setting sun served as her guide home.

It was time to go. That was the rule her parents had drummed into her: *Always turn your back to the sunset and walk east toward the castle.*

Everyone surmised that a night-time forest was a dangerous place. Tatiana had no reason to believe otherwise because she always followed that one rule—if few others. Today she felt the streak of rebellion that frazzled the servants and sometimes, when he noticed, her father—lord of the castle. Perhaps it was his absence on a rare trip to over-see the fiefdom's distant villages that had stirred her muti-nous mood.

She dawdled. Barely noticed when a sudden breeze again stirred the leaves. Disregarded signs that something was not right in her forest solace.

The breeze stiffened to a loud wind, startling Tatiana enough to get her to look at the birch trunks bending as if in prayer before her.

Something was happening. She could not fathom what. Within seconds, a huge shadow loomed over the treetops. She had no idea what it might be, other than that it was shaped like an oversize version of something she'd seen many times: a mortar. From inside it a smaller pestle-like shadow stirred clouds rather than pounded herbs or spices.

Then it was gone. She imagined she heard a loud cackle, like that of an enormous chicken.

All returned to silence.

Tatiana stood and gathered her collection of forest find-ings before she began to walk briskly east. She didn't know what she'd seen. However, for the first time in her ten and seven years, she suspected it had something to do with the witch she truly hadn't believed existed.

The witch had a name. A name so powerful no one would mention it except in whispers. Tatiana's mother had seldom uttered it. However, Tatiana never took seriously tales and rumors that abounded in the village about a fearsome and powerful woman who allegedly gobbled up small children.

Yet today she knew she had seen something. Or someone. Could it have something to do with the witch? The forbidden name echoed in her mind all the way back to the castle: *Baba Yaga.*

***

"Have you heard the news?" her lady greeted her excitedly when Tatiana returned from the courtyard alcove where she'd hidden her official women's clothing.

Relieved no one had chided her for lateness, Tatiana obediently raised her arms so Olga could slip off that same gown and replace it with something more suitable for dining.

"I really don't need to be so formal, since I plan to eat in the kitchen," Tatiana protested, though her breach of etiquette garnered no response. She sighed. "So, what is this big news?"

Olga paused to cross herself. She seemed as breathless as Tatiana felt.

"My Lady Tanya, you have missed all the happenings in the tsardom! The princess is dead!"

Tatiana stared blankly at the woman who had been her childhood nurse and now lady's maid. Her mind remained filled with what she imagined she'd seen in the forest.

"What?"

"Our beloved princess, the love of the tsarevich's life, is gone! They say the Tsarevna Natalya Sergeievna coughed once, and then fell down dead."

"That's . . . that's awful."

"Tis so. Everyone knows it was a true love match. And now she is gone to heaven, just like that."

Tatiana tried to feign interest as she hurried to the kitchen to dine. If the servants felt any discomfort with the informality of sharing their space with the lord's daughter, she did not care. Eating alone at a lengthy table presided over by the empty chair where her father usually sat was not her idea of enjoying a meal.

The cook Maria and her assistant Masha hastened to set her a place, and Tatiana settled into a plain wooden chair at a plain wooden table rather than surrounded by the dining room's elegant furnishings.

The two women barely noticed. They could speak of nothing other than the mysterious and sudden death of the tsarevich's wife, Tsarevna Natalya or, as she was often called, Princess Natalya Sergeievna. The second part of her second name, per the custom, was based on that of her father, Sergei.

Tanya, whose father was named Nicholas, was called Lady Tatiana Nicholaevna Tolkov; few people used surnames.

"It is incredibly sad," Cook Maria said, crossing herself.

Tatiana bit her lip to keep from grinning at all these displays of piety, and merely nodded. She listened to gossip out of habit, although the lives of royals who lived far away in the vast empire of Rus did not matter to her.

"And they say," the cook continued, "that the old tsar is frequently ill and thus his son the tsarevich might inherit the throne soon. Now the heir has no mother, no wife, and just a young girl to care for."

"My father says it would take weeks to get to the capital by boat and horse," Tatiana mentioned.

The women nodded, then continued their discussion.

"And now who will look out for Snow?" Masha asked Maria.

"Snow?" Tatiana interrupted.

"My lady, the little grand duchess is the second love of His Highness's life," Maria said.

"Of course."

"They call her *Sneg* or Snow. Her real name is Snowdrop," Masha chimed in. "Their highnesses always doted on the poor child. How will she get along without her mother?"

Tatiana ate slowly, savoring the thin pancakes called *blini,* stuffed this evening with fresh forest mushrooms and the villagers' cheese. She should feel a bit sad for Snowdrop. Nevertheless, her mind was on other matters.

"I have heard things about the young princess," Cook Maria whispered. Snow's official title was grand duchess, yet everyone referred to her as princess, just like her late mother.

And then they moved out of the kitchen before Tatiana could hear exactly what things the cook had heard.

She shrugged and finished her ice cream. Being motherless herself, she could feel badly for the tsarevich and his daughter—the little princess who, if not for her gender, would be second in line for the throne of the principality of Muscovy and the tsardom of Rus. She had never seen these people, though, and their troubles had nothing to do with her life.

Tatiana had *other* worries, such as the potential arrival in *her* forest of a witch.

She knew the local priest insisted there was no such thing. In all other matters the church was the last word. Yet most people knew what they knew: Baba Yaga was real, and Tatiana now suspected they all were right.

Chapter 2

Two weeks later, Tatiana still had not returned to her beloved forest. She told herself she was needed at the castle. However, matters generally ran well on those rare occasions her father departed to tour outlying villages and farms whose residents paid rents and obeisance to their lord.

Mostly the servants carried on with their duties, interrupted occasionally by suggestions from the young lady only unofficially in charge. When Tatiana mentioned that the drapes seemed heavier than usual with dust, someone cleaned them. If she noted the slight blackening on a silver tray, it received a polish. On mornings when the cook remembered to consult her about the day's menu, she offered her opinion. If she felt really rebellious, she ordered red caviar made from the roe of salmon who jumped the waterfall in the nearby river.

Some afternoons Tatiana strolled slowly through the village, dispensing a kind word to the shopkeepers and a bright greeting to those mingling at the market. Sometimes she dug out coins to purchase things no one wanted; still, they might help keep various merchants in business.

Today she needed a few items, so she started with the candlemaker. He seemed distracted, smiling politely at his lady as he handed her the two fat candles she had purchased before turning to the baker next door. They resumed their conversation, which seemed to be the same one everyone was having.

"The poor prince," the baker said.

"*Da*. Tis true the tsarevich will mourn for years," agreed the candlemaker.

"They say he may remarry soon anyway," the woman putting finishing touches of frosting on a cake whispered loudly.

"Truly?"

"He knows he needs another heir."

"It's sad that his poor little motherless daughter cannot inherit . . ."

"The tsarevich having a girl is not the main problem, you see. It's that they say she is—"

Both stopped talking and looked uneasily at Tatiana. "May I help you with anything else, My Lady?" the candlemaker asked.

"No, I'm fine. What is wrong with the child?"

"Nothing," he said quickly.

"Aye, nothing, My Lady," echoed the baker. "Would you like some fresh black bread?"

Tatiana pulled out another coin, knowing full well that the

castle kitchens contained plenty of loaves of various breads.

At the bookseller's she asked if they had a collection of folktales that might include stories about Baba Yaga. She imagined such a book thick with tales like those her mother had been writing by hand at her death.

"*Nyet!*" the bookseller cried, acting as offended as if she had demanded to acquire his entire manuscript collection without paying one ruble for it.

"I can read French," she offered confidently.

"My Lady, please do not ask for such a thing that does not exist."

"I thought—"

The man, dressed in the traditional kaftan or coat that fell to his ankles, appeared almost frightened as he leaned closer to her. "Please, My Lady. I do not wish for trouble. The Patriarch strictly prohibits such writings."

"I see." She should have known that, since the church insisted on publishers only printing books from the Bible and occasional historical accounts in the Russian language. Certain acceptable books printed in French and Latin were available.

Disappointed, she curled up on a velvet settee in one of the castle turrets' round rooms. Her mother had completed over one hundred painstaking pages in tight, elegant French script she'd learned from her own father. Most villagers could neither read nor write. Tatiana's mother had insisted on hiring a tutor, Sonya Ivanovna, to do the same for her daughter as her father had done for her.

In between tales that Tatiana had ignored for years, she carefully set down the rapidly fading pages and glanced below at the ships sailing the river behind the semi-fortified castle.

Father will be coming home soon, she told herself, squinting at the horizon and wishing for the twentieth time that she could have sailed away with him. Although she admitted to herself that she feared being afloat on the water, she wanted to see a little of what awaited beyond the realm of Tolkov Castle.

"Your own travel days await you," her father had assured her when she had asked to accompany him. "For now, however, I need someone to stay here lest anything happens."

Nothing ever did happen. At least so it seemed to Tatiana, who had to admit she did not want to go away for a long period. Only a few days perhaps. Just enough to see what was around the riverbend.

As days passed and Tatiana devoured most of the fairytales for the second and then third time, she savored the accounts of firebirds, Princess Vasilissa and Prince Ivan's adventures, talking horses, flying wolves, and magical protectives. She knew some tsars were wicked, and some benevolent (she had no idea into which category the kingdom's current tsar or his son the tsarevich fit and resolved to ask Sonya). Above all, she read and reread a lot more about Baba Yaga, whose hut apparently stood on chicken legs and who sometimes consumed and other times pardoned children who wandered into her forest domain. On the other hand, unless horses really could talk and wolves could fly, there was little chance that the witch of the fairytales really existed.

By the time her father did return, loaded with gifts for everyone and stories of his encounters, Tatiana had forgiven him for not taking her along.

"My beloved daughter," he greeted her. "It has been far too long. I've missed you and promise next time you may accompany me."

"Thank you, father. I shall be happy to do so, despite not liking to go so far away for so long." She had worn her best sarafan—a flowing floor-length dress over a linen blouse—for his return. He invited her to twirl around and show off her finery.

"You look lovely," he commented. "Just as beautiful as your dear mother was." After wiping surreptitiously at his eyes, he added, "Soon we should find you a husband."

"I will stay here with you and my forest forever," she vowed.

He laughed. "What nonsense is this? A young lady of nearly eighteen years clinging to the villagers' ways and wandering the countryside the way you did as a child?"

"I am your creature of the forest, father. Remember when you used to call me so?"

Nicholas Ivanovich Tolkov tugged at his auburn beard, longer and bushier after his travels. As a child, Tatiana had pulled on it mercilessly, admiring the way it glistened in the sun in shades of crimson, cinnamon, and scarlet. Today for the first time she noticed threads of gray amidst the reds.

"I do remember. And your mother and I taught you what we knew about the woods. However, perhaps now it is time you learned more about indoor activities."

"Please, father. Do not make me cook. Or sew."

He laughed again. "No, my dearest. I fear you will always need servants for those tasks. No one will ever forget your famous fallen souffle or your frock with sleeves of two vastly different lengths. Unless," he teased, "you would like to try again at perfecting those skills?"

"Never, I guarantee you. I *would* like more practice with the bow when you have time to accompany me." She smiled back, assured she would never again be forced to knead bread dough or hem gowns, tasks her father knew she detested.

"Very well," he said, his face growing serious. "However, I do believe it is time you became more involved in the running of our holdings and also in hosting our guests rather than spending every minute you are not at your lessons wandering the forest."

So he *had* noticed her absences before he left.

"Father—"

"Nonnegotiable," he insisted.

"I *do* want to sit with you during court briefings," she admitted. "And perhaps only a couple hours a day in the forest?"

"Done. Now off to bed with you."

She rose from the dining room table, curtsied, and kissed her father lightly on the forehead. "Good night, sire."

That night she burned an entire candle reading her mother's manuscript pages before slipping out of bed and removing a small item from her bureau drawer. Olga had left her clothing for the next day on the chair, and Tatiana tucked the item into the pouch she always took with her to the forest.

She would obey her father despite missing her long woodland afternoons. Soon she would return to the forest. Surely if there had been a witch there, she had moved on by now.

Tatiana had told no one, including her father, about the shadow or silhouette she imagined she'd seen. Who would believe her? And if anyone did, it was a certainty her father would forbid her from going into the forest entirely rather than permitting a few hours.

***

Mornings Tatiana worked diligently on the lessons delivered by Sonya, who insisted her young charge memorize the anatomy of the human body, the star constellations, and the geographical features of the entire kingdom of Rus—the sprawling territory ruled by the tsar. Afternoons were reserved for homework, reading, and French and Latin practice. Sometimes Igor, the local healer, gave her lessons in herbal remedies.

Now she added helping her father to her studies. He'd kept his promise, inviting her to sit beside him as he dispensed justice when disputes arose among the tenants. She found she enjoyed it, and quickly learned how to look up dates and land deeds in the thick parchment books that had served as the castle's records for centuries.

A day arrived when Tatiana was desperate to return to her favorite place. After the sun shone straight overhead, she leisurely picked her way across a forest floor now carpeted with ruby- and topaz-colored leaves.

If Baba Yaga really did exist, Tatiana resolved not to flee, no matter how long it took for her to find the sun in the west. The autumn winds and rain had removed half of the leaves and she might be able to see something untoward more clearly. Something or someone, she thought a bit nervously, patting the grass ahead with her gold-knobbed walking stick.

She followed the left fork of her favorite path, finding it slightly more overgrown than on her last visit. Yet the deer and an occasional moose or elk kept it wide enough for her to walk, and she tapped the ground to scare off any snakes potentially lingering into the autumn months. Ahead she would find her favorite meadow, the one where she often encountered does and their fawns, who occasionally albeit rarely permitted her to pet them.

As she emerged from the path, she stopped short so fast she tumbled onto the leaf-strewn, muddy path. Rolling over, she quickly regained her feet.

At the opposite end of the grassy clearing stood what she recognized instantly from her mother's written descriptions: a huge thatched-roof hut that seemed to wobble on its perch atop two thick-as-elm trunk legs. Actual chicken legs. Giant ones.

Amazed and frightened, she hurried to take cover behind the vibrant red and orange flaming foliage in a copse of sumac lining the path opening. She could neither allow herself to be seen, nor force herself to turn and flee. She merely gazed open-mouthed at the sight before her.

No smoke rose from the hut's lopsided chimney. The door, which she couldn't make out clearly, appeared closed. Extending out from the hut's legs, a fence made of what could only be bones encircled a large area. At this distance, she could just make out skulls sticking up every meter or so from the fence's posts.

Tatiana shivered, pulling her autumn cloak around herself. Was the witch at home? Would she see—or smell—a new human presence so close to her?

She waited, peering through the sumac so long her eyes watered. Nothing happened. The chicken legs did not move in her direction. The chimney still did not emit the smoke one expected on such a chilly day. No giant mortar and pestle occupied the outdoor premises.

Considering herself fortunate beyond belief, Tatiana backed up slowly and dared to survey behind herself. To the right a red glow identified the setting sun. This meant she could escape east without passing the hut. She would turn and slip quietly through the trees back to the edge of the forest that emerged near the castle. Forgetting her earlier brave resolutions, she moved away stealthily and noiselessly as possible. As soon as she'd put some distance between herself and what was indisputably Baba Yaga's hut, she ran.

Sneaking along hedges that blocked the view from villagers, a breathless Tatiana found her way into the tiny alcove near the castle's back entrance. Here she removed her cloak. She expertly replaced the groomsman's tunic and breeches she preferred to wear with the sarafan she'd worn to her lessons earlier. She even hid the cane here.

Her curiosity was more than satisfied. She chided herself for being so foolish, resolving not to return until she was completely convinced the witch no longer inhabited this particular forest. If her mother had been right after all, the witch lived "everywhere and nowhere," and the latter worked for her.

Chapter 3

Just before dawn a few weeks later, a grim-faced Olga awakened her. "You must come at once!"

"What is it?" Tatiana responded sleepily.

"No time!" Olga insisted when Tatiana reached for a wrap to cover her nightgown.

Her first thought was the witch. Baba Yaga had been on her mind ever since she'd spied the hut. Had the witch somehow entered the village or, worse yet, the palace? Should she, Tatiana, have warned someone? She hadn't, and now anything that happened would be her fault!

"It's your father," Olga said breathlessly, holding a candle high as they hurried along the corridor leading to the opposite side of the palace.

"What's wrong?"

"He is ill," Olga yelled over her shoulder.

"What's wrong with him?" Surely it must be serious if she had been summoned wearing only her night clothes by the usually decorous Olga.

Olga did not respond until they reached Lord Nicholas's chambers. Igor, the healer, stood over the bed, trying to coax his patient to sip some kind of liquid.

"Father!"

He leaned slightly forward from his reclining position, giving her a wan smile. "I am fine, dearest daughter. All is well."

Igor stared unblinkingly at her and his eyes did not echo that prognosis.

"What is wrong?" she demanded, putting out her hand to hold that of her father. She addressed her question to Igor.

The man with a long vee-shaped gray beard and matching eyebrows set down the spoon and laid a presumably cold cloth over his patient's temple. "Perhaps the weather. Perhaps indigestion. Perhaps nothing serious."

"Or *perhaps* something more serious?" On most days she admired and trusted Igor, though this time his diagnostic failure frustrated her.

She sat on the edge of the bed and grasped her father's warm hand. Too warm.

"Child!" Olga protested. "It might be something that could spread to you."

"It's not. And I'm not a child."

"My Lady, you must be more careful," Olga chided.

"I *am* careful," She settled herself more firmly on the canopied bed's mattress and reached for her father's face. Just that fast he'd fallen asleep.

She fixed her greenish eyes on Igor. "What did you give him?"

At first the healer ignored her, then replied, "Just some tea—and a dose of bitter root."

"What are his symptoms?"

"Stomach pains. And as you can tell, he has a high fever."

This sounded more serious than indigestion, and she told Igor so.

"Pardon me, My Lady," he said more gently. "All the knowledge you have gained under my tutelage still does not qualify you to identify or cure illnesses. Would you agree?"

She had to admit it was so, though nonetheless fretted over her own helplessness.

"Have you tried birch bark?"

"I have. Now, My Lady, we must allow him to sleep. For hours if he needs it. It is the ultimate cure for all illnesses."

Again, Tatiana had to agree. Still, she refused to return to her own chambers to dress for breaking her fast until afternoon sunshine slanted through the slatted window.

Still her father had not awakened.

And so it went, with the fever refusing to diminish for days. And days. Lord Nicholas awoke only occasionally to sip some of the cook's chicken broth or Igor's latest concoction before falling asleep again.

Igor spent hours in the dispensary searching his manuscripts for possible cures, moving aside silently when Tatiana started joining him. Yet nothing they read or tried worked. Together they took turns grinding herbs. Mixing concoctions. Pounding powders. Searching the castle's herb gardens for fresh ingredients.

Alas, not a single remedy had any effect.

Lord Nicholas did manage to speak when he awakened, albeit only to assure them he would be "fine."

His fever eventually broke. The stomach pains, however, persisted.

Meanwhile, Tatiana found that the lord's duties often needed attending, unlike when he had had the opportunity to arrange all his matters before traveling. She began to occupy the receiving room each morning, dealing diligently with villagers' and servants' needs, requests, demands, and disputes that her father would normally oversee.

At times she enjoyed the work, despite not being able to wait to turn such tasks back over to her father. True, unless he remarried in the future and had more children, this might be her own future. Women did manage estates if their husbands died, and Tolkov Castle's subjects were accustomed to her already. On the other hand, this was not something she wanted to contemplate.

Tatiana did not want to marry. She did not necessarily want a stepmother, either. She desired only one thing: her father's full recovery.

An entire month passed the same way. Each afternoon she sat with Lord Nicholas, and then found her way to the village church where she prayed and lit a candle at each of several icons.

Yet neither prayers nor herbs seemed to work.

By now the snow had filled the moat and the outlying land, with villagers barely able to move their sleighs and troikas through the drifts. It all seemed too silent, as if the entire countryside held its breath awaiting the lord's recovery.

It took Tatiana a long time to realize what she had to do.

She'd read all the tales of Baba Yaga, enough to know that the witch was famous for two things: her embroideries and her herbal remedies. She had no choice. She had to return to the forest and pray that the woman who resided in the hut on chicken legs had remained there for the winter.

***

This time no one could detect that she wore breeches, let alone fur-covered ones. Over them she donned her least favorite fur cloak, accompanied by a rabbit fur muff, hat, gloves, and boots made from seal skins. Lastly, she picked up the small leather pouch she always carried outside, checked to ensure it still contained the small item she kept in her drawer, and sneaked past a snoozing Olga and through the empty kitchen.

She soon found herself taking high steps to get through the heavy snow that led to the forest entrance.

Without the familiar trails to follow, Tatiana had great difficulty locating the clearing where the hut had stood months earlier. By the time she did, frost coated her eyelids and tendrils of reddish hair.

Smoke curled upwards from the chimney, and the windows seemed transformed into eyes that glared at her. Beside the hut stood a tall cauldron Tatiana knew Baba would use to fly from place to place.

Traipsing through the clearing and approaching the fence—barely coated with snow though lit with flaming skulls—she realized from her anatomy lessons that the fence had been created out of a combination of femur and tibia bones. The fence posts resembled hip bones. She shivered from more than the cold before she reached for the gate.

As if belatedly, the hut seemed to sense her presence. It squawked.

Within seconds the chicken legs left the ground as the entire hut lifted and twirled around, the door now facing the forest and away from its reluctant yet desperate guest.

Fortunately, Tatiana knew what to do from the stories. As she got within shouting distance of the back of the hut, she cried out, "Little hut, little hut! Turn your back to the forest and your front to me!"

Nothing happened.

She tried again, cupping her mouth with her gloved hands:

"Little hut, little hut! Turn your back to the forest
and your front to me!"

The hut once again lifted. This time it spun around with blood-curdling screeches and loud creakings before facing the girl in furs.

Seconds later, a wooden staircase dropped from the doorway to the snow-covered ground, right between the chicken legs' clawed feet.

Relieved though still terrified, Tatiana moved forward. She removed her hat and shook out her hair, her eyes never leaving the door with jawbone latches and an open-mouthed handle as it inched its way open.

A wizened hand reached out and beckoned her forward. Heart in her throat, Tatiana closed the now shrieking gate behind her, moved toward the hut, then grasped the ladder and climbed to the doorway.

Inside, she could hardly breathe. Not only was she nervous, the hut was smoldering hot. In addition to a cauldron atop a cast-iron stove fueled by logs, tongues of flame rose from a fireplace. A huge loom dominated one corner.

In an armchair beside the fireplace sat a crone, her waist-length silver hair cascading over her shoulders and down to her breasts. Her face resembled a dry creek bed, cracked into myriad pieces. Atop her head rose a horn made of bone.

"Good afternoon," Tatiana managed to utter, realizing immediately that she must have made a huge mistake putting herself in this much danger. *How can I heal my father if I never get out of here, never return from the forest?*

"*Devushka*. Young lady! How dare you enter my domain? Have you no idea who I am?"

"Yes, Your—Your Grace. I know it well."

"Fortunately, you have arrived in time for dinner." The crone beckoned her closer.

For a moment Tatiana felt relieved. She was to be welcomed. Her mother had assured her that she need only be kind to the witch.

Maybe not. As she saw the woman devour her with glittering blue eyes and then glance hungrily at the cauldron bubbling on the stove, realization dawned.

Baba Yaga didn't mean to invite her to dine. She meant that she, Tatiana, was to *be* the dinner!

"Your Grace—"

"Enough! Call me Baba or grandmother. I am not some ridiculous human royal."

"Grandmother, my name is Tanya. I am not here to satisfy your appetite, only to beg a huge favor."

"Take off that awful coat. And I don't grant favors to my dinner dishes." Baba Yaga's voice sounded shrill and reedy, yet her eyes remained incongruously warm.

Tatiana did not want to remove her coat, taking her time hanging it over the chair opposite Baba and then daring to take a seat there herself. She was exhausted from fighting the deep snow drifts and figured at this point she had little to lose by offending someone who planned to salt and pepper her before serving her up with beets and potatoes.

Baba did not seem to notice. She stood, revealing a lanky, bony-legged figure wearing a plain knee-length burgundy dress and worn buckled shoes. Around her neck dangled necklaces interspersed with miniature skulls. She reached for a book beside the stove.

Tatiana tried again. "I'm just—"

"Quiet!" the witch interrupted. "Now, let us consult the book."

She remained silent as ordered while Baba sat back down and flipped through pages, muttering aloud as she encountered what sounded like horrifying recipes.

"Let's see here," she repeated before reading aloud. "Maiden *mignon*. Hash-browned hands with porridge. *Nyet*, I had that last time. Well then, perhaps appendix on rye. It's just a sandwich. I am not *that* hungry."

Tatiana swallowed hard, then noticed a stack of journals and books piled on the floor beside Baba. These titles she could read: *Heavenly Hair Recipes. Seven Ways to Sweeten Bone Stew. Ten Tips for Tastier Toes.*

"If—if I could just show you," she stammered bravely.

"Show me? Show me how plump you are *not*, do you mean?" Baba Yaga marked her place in the cookbook and looked hard at her again.

"Yes, I'm thin. Too thin for eating. I think I'd taste tough."

"It's only a sandwich."

"But—"

"Before my appetite comes back, perhaps you can do some chores around here. They say no one cleans like a virgin." Her eyes narrowed. "You *are* a virgin, are you not? Otherwise . . . well, otherwise we shall have to find some other use for you."

"Yes, I am. A virgin, I mean." Tatiana could feel herself blush, no doubt reddening her already chafed skin more.

"Excellent. Now, I have dusting to be done." She pointed one sharpened finger toward a row of empty vessels. "And pots to wipe. Certainly you can handle that."

"I've never done either of those things, Grandmother."

"*Oy.* How tragic. Well, now you will learn. Get started, whatever your name is. Not that it matters."

"I'm Tanya. Tanya Nicholaevna from the Tolkov Castle. And my father, Nicholas Tolkov, is—"

"Begin! Here is the cloth. All my dolls require dusting."

For the first time Tatiana noticed the rack of *matryoshka* or nesting dolls lined up in a corner cupboard opposite the loom. Inside each one would be a dozen or so more dolls, each subsequently smaller than the one before it.

"I'd be happy to. In fact, Your . . . I mean Baba, I have one of my own *matryoshka* dolls that I brought to show you." She reached into her pouch just as Baba held up one withered hand with talon-like fingernails.

"*Nyet*! I don't want to see it!"

"It is a gift from my late mother!"

"It is a damn blessing from her, you mean."

"Perhaps it is. She gave me the doll and blessed me with it a couple years before she died."

"A dead mother? That is thrice thirty times worse."

"*Da*, she is gone from me. And if I do not get your assistance, my father may die, too." Tatiana no longer felt afraid, just desperate to accomplish her errand.

After weeping for a couple moments, she realized Baba Yaga had abandoned her chair and returned with a cup of tea from a copper samovar opposite the nested dolls. "Drink this, child. And no crying in my home. I don't allow it."

"I'm sorry, Grandmother. My Lord Tolkov is seriously ill, and his death would be tragic for the entire surrounding fiefdom. Not to mention make me an orphan."

"Pooh! What is wrong with him?"

"He had a high fever. Now, however, he mainly complains of griping in his guts. Pains that prevent him from getting out of bed."

"I see." Baba pulled out a long clay pipe with an amber bowl. She lit it with one finger before raising it to her chapped lips. "Well, I cannot dine on someone who possesses a mother's blessing. A *father's* blessing is fine. However, I do, of course, know a bit about healing herbs."

"The stories about you all insist you know more about them than anyone in all of Rus."

Baba seemed pleased. She grinned, revealing a set of iron teeth with sharpened fangs and bicuspids. Tatiana had a feeling she knew exactly what had gnawed all the meat off the bones in the yard.

"If the storytellers sing about me, it must be true," Baba said, and Tatiana did not correct her. "Let me see what I have. Go to the stove and help yourself to some cheese pies and pickles, girl."

"Thank you, Grandmother."

While she sat in the chair savoring *zakuski,* or appetizers, Tatiana watched Baba pull out a mortar and then a sack full of herbs and foliage. She rifled through the sack before extracting something that smelled pungent from across the room. Within minutes she produced an elaborately carved pestle and began grinding at the plant. When she had finished, she slid the powder into a glass vial.

"There you go. Put this with your doll."

"Do you not want the doll yourself? I brought it for you."

"You brought it to interfere! Just take the remedy and put a little each night into his porridge or soup. He will be cured in three nights time. And do not tell anyone where you received this gift."

"What is in it?"

"I do not share my potions or healing remedies. Don't ask so many questions. I repeat: do not tell *anyone!*"

"I won't. I cannot thank you enough, Grandmother."

"You will thank me again when you return. I do not doubt that I have other things you will need in the future. Magic items," she added somewhat slyly.

"But—"

"But nothing. I will remain here only until after the lilacs finish blooming and the earth turns fertile for planting. Then

I must move on. Therefore, you should return soon." She emphasized the last word.

"Yes, Grandmother." Tatiana crossed her fingers behind herself, certain she would never dare return.

"Remember: I know more about your life than anyone, and you will need what I have to give you should you be forced to travel."

"This is more than enough . . ."

"Just remember," Baba repeated, and then set down her pipe and opened the door. A burst of arctic air blew inside. "Now go! It grows dark."

Indeed it had, and Tatiana fled down the rickety staircase, through the yard, out the bone gate, and into the clearing.

She followed her own tracks all the way home.

Chapter 4

Four days later, Lord Nicholas Ivanovich Tolkov left his bed and returned to his former daily routine. No one remarked that his daughter had volunteered to serve him the cook's special *borsch* for the past three nights.

To give thanks, the castle occupants and the villagers took turns kneeling before the church's icons. Tatiana joined them.

Lord Tolkov and his daughter Lady Tatiana also celebrated by inviting everyone who could trudge through the snow to attend a special banquet in the castle's ballroom. Since nearly half the year was spent in a white and icy world, the villagers were thrilled to gather around massive fireplaces and dine on roasted venison, hare, pheasant, goose, and duck. The leftover food went home in full sacks.

Because the river had iced over as usual and deep drifts

blocked the mountain passes in all directions, word from the outside world seldom reached them in the winter. By early spring, however, the castle and its vassals began to look forward to the return of its three knights—called bogatyrs. These strong warriors—Sir Igor, Sir Dimitri, and Sir Mikhail—also happened to be Nicholas's cousins, and served as the fiefdom's liaisons to the tsar. Equally adept at swordplay and archery, they also defended the castle during the summer months. They had left for the capital of Moskva the previous summer, and, as usual, returned when the snow melted, the passes cleared, and the rivers thawed.

Tatiana had followed the bogatyrs' route for years, as Sonya delighted in pulling out large maps from Lord Nicholas's library. If Tatiana had any interest in visiting such faraway places, she had always assumed it would be in the distant future.

This changed when the bogatyrs returned.

***

"We have a proclamation from the tsar," Sir Dimitri announced when the three appeared in the receiving room to offer their winter report to Lord Nicholas. They wore heavy, red wool kaftans, high black boots, and pointed fur hats.

"Of course you do," Nicholas greeted them before signaling to the hovering servants. "Get these men ale and bread. News has waited all these months, and it certainly can await a fine meal for such brave men."

Tatiana was permitted to join her father, whose brush with death had impressed upon them both a sense of urgency about the future of the fiefdom. Since Lord Nicholas still lacked any interest in remarrying, his daughter might become the sole ruler sooner than either of them had foreseen. In the provinces, unlike the princedoms, this likely would be permitted regardless of her gender.

Without preamble, Sir Igor announced, "His imperial majesty the tsar wishes the widowed tsarevich to find a new bride as soon as possible."

"He wants all eligible maidens in the realm to present themselves no later than early August," Sir Mikhail continued. "This will allow them to get to the capital for the bride selection process."

Then Sir Dimitri read the official declaration.

At first Tatiana listened with only mild interest, assuming the biggest news from Moskva and the tsar would have little to do with her.

Then the import of the proclamation sunk in for both her and her father.

"You mean my only daughter and heir is summoned to the capital?" Lord Nicholas asked incredulously.

"Yes, My Lord. All unmarried women of the nobility must begin their travels immediately."

It was as if a large stone had lodged itself in Tatiana's stomach. She would not go!

"It is not possible!" she protested when she regained her breath and stomach.

"*Nyet*, it is not!" Lord Nicholas informed the three men who had assembled after their meal.

"My Lord," Sir Igor said. "There is no choice in the matter. The names and ranks of all the available noblewomen are in the records. The tsar's ministers will know it well if my lady does not appear."

"She is needed here!"

"There is a penalty," Sir Mikhail said quietly. "The pillory or the knout, if not imprisonment for any noble family who refuses."

"The selection process is a great honor," Sir Dimitri added.

Mikhail nodded his proud head. "The women who do not suit the tsarevich will return the following summer at the latest. Only one woman—the one he chooses—must stay behind."

"One out of hundreds, perhaps thousands," Sir Igor reiterated.

"Then I will go," Tatiana said suddenly. Perhaps the time for her to travel had arrived, and most assuredly she would return in autumn.

Her father frowned. "You know nothing of the habits of such people, my dear daughter. They do not do things the way we do them here. You will be miserable."

Sir Mikhail knelt before him. "Cousin, I will accompany my lady to the capital. No harm will come to her." The other two knights agreed to the journey as well.

"It is not physical harm that I worry about. I have heard much about the lives of the women in the royal palaces. They live as prisoners in special rooms called terems, and my daughter is accustomed to a life of freedom."

"We will take care of her," Sir Mikhail repeated. "We vow to return her safely to you next spring at the latest."

Lord Nicholas scowled. "See that you do so, or you shall lose your swords and your ranks."

And so it was decided.

***

Tatiana had no desire to marry, a fact she had repeatedly impressed upon her father. As for love and romance, opportunities were scarce here, with the exception of a few lackluster suitors. They inevitably had presented themselves to her father in hopes of forging a partnership that would include birch timber from the forests he ruled. This Lord Tolkov refused to trade, and Tatiana made no secret of her delight. It angered her when anyone suggested stripping the forests of their beauty, moreso to imagine herself married off.

She had no intention of changing her mind now. Luckily, the hordes of women who would flock to the capital provided a guarantee that she herself would return to Tolkov Castle within a year at most.

Nevertheless, over the next few weeks of preparation, Tatiana sighed frequently, picked at her meals, and sulked whenever Sonya or Olga tried to get a response from her.

She vehemently wished to stay, despite her duty being to go. So go she would.

Packing was accomplished in record time, albeit for an entire week they awaited completion of the gowns ordered from local dressmakers. Their lady could not possibly show up at the tsar's palace without fashionable sarafans and robes that gave a good impression, making her castle and lord appear prosperous.

There was one day remaining, and Tatiana already had spent most of her precious remaining time with her father, who bravely hid his angst at her departure. They might not see one another for months or up to a year.

She had not forgotten about Baba Yaga, and found herself thinking frequently about the witch's insistence that she return to the hut where she had been given a cure for her father. Now it was late spring, and there was no guarantee the witch and her hut would still be in Tolkov Castle's forest.

Yet Tatiana knew she had to try.

Spring had come to the forest in a dazzling array of newly budded trees and bushes. Crocuses and tiny cupped snowdrops peeked out beneath leftover snow. No lilacs had opened as yet. "After the lilacs begin to bloom," Baba had said. She should still be there.

She was.

Tatiana stood at the edge of the clearing occupied by the hut. She remained there for an hour, awaiting a glimpse of the witch. She believed she owed it to Baba to thank her for Lord Nicholas's remarkable recovery, although truly feared she might not escape this second encounter with the witch.

As if she could smell Tatiana, Baba emerged from the door high atop her hut's chicken legs. When she beckoned before going back inside, Tatiana knew the gesture was meant for her.

Unlike on the previous occasion, the hut stayed facing forward, as if expecting her. The stairs dropped down as before, and she climbed them nervously. She noticed that the hut's door latch seemed comprised of metatarsal or finger bones.

"You took many months," Baba greeted her sternly.

"I am sorry, Grandmother. The snow kept me inside throughout winter," Tatiana only partially lied.

"Your father survived." Baba said it firmly, as if there was no question.

"Yes. I cannot thank you enough for your cure. It worked marvelously."

Baba waved as if to dismiss the thanks, seeming pleased with herself nonetheless. "Of course."

Tatiana did not know how to ask for what she wanted. She pulled the little nesting doll her mother had bestowed from the pouch, once again intending to offer it to Baba.

"Put that away!"

"Grandmother—"

"I told you last time I do not deal in blessings."

"You did tell me so. I only intended—"

"*I* dispense the gifts."

"Yes, Grandmother."

"Now, sit."

The hut looked exactly as she remembered, and Tatiana knew which chair not to take. She settled into the one she had occupied a few months ago and waited.

"You are going on a journey," Baba stated flatly.

"How—how did you know?"

Baba waved a hand in dismissal. "I have two items for you to pack."

"Items?"

The witch reached into a sack near the fireplace and pulled out a tiny vial that she then handed to her. Tatiana reached out, trying not to think about the way Baba's fingernails looked sharp and pointed as one of the cook's knives.

"It is a potion."

"A potion? For inducing love?" Tatiana had read of such

things, and heard them whispered about by the village girls. Perhaps Baba wanted her to attract the tsarevich's attention.

"This is much more important! If you suspect poison, you must put two drops on your tongue to counteract it."

"Poison?" What could this be about? What did poisons have to do with her own life?

"Just keep it," Baba insisted, watching while Tatiana slipped the innocuous bottle into her pouch. "There is more."

Tatiana started to sweat, realizing that despite the warm temperature outside, the fireplace burned brightly inside.

This time Baba produced a lavishly decorated handheld mirror. "For warnings," she said simply.

"Warnings?"

"You shall find its use when it is most needed."

The mirror barely fit, though Tatiana dutifully forced it into her pouch.

"Now it is time for tea." Baba rose and moved to the samovar; then, as if by magic, she turned back to offer her guest a tray covered with tiny cucumber and radish sandwiches, strawberry strudel, and pastries topped with whipped vanilla frosting and raisins.

Tatiana ate quickly, intending to flee as soon as it seemed polite.

Then, realizing anew that she was in a powerful presence, she dared to ask questions.

"Do you know when I shall return to this forest? Can you see into the future?"

Baba grinned, an expression that rippled her skin folds and reminded Tatiana of the furrows in nearby fields at planting time. "We are abandoning this forest, you and I."

"Yes, I intend to depart for the capital in the morning."

Baba shrugged. "Go then, *devushka*. Go and remember: morning is always wiser than the evening."

"It is?"

The tray and tea seemed to disappear on their own, and Baba turned away and buried herself in a book. Tatiana realized that her visit had concluded.

On the way home she collected fresh plants and herbs for the journey. She also paused so that a family of rabbits could nibble blades of grass from her hands.

She would miss the forest and its inhabitants. She might, unbelievably, miss Baba. For now, though, she had so much more to think about.

Chapter 5

After a brief appearance at her own farewell party, Tatiana hugged her father tightly and said her goodbyes to most of the staff. She would depart before sunrise.

In addition to the three knights, she was to be accompanied by her tutor Sonya, her lady's maid Olga, and the cook's assistant Masha. Cook Maria, as well as the huntsmen, groomsmen, and other servants, would stay behind to tend Lord Nicholas and the castle. The three selected women appeared as nervous as Tatiana, albeit much more excited. Like their lady, none of the three had left this castle home in their lives. Unlike their lady, the servants viewed the journey as the ultimate adventure.

Which it probably was, Tatiana thought as she watched them climb into a boat that would sail to a designated meeting place in the faraway city of Yaroslavl. Tatiana and her "guards," needing horses for the remainder of the trip, would travel overland for the coming days and weeks.

At first she and her father's cousins encountered nothing more interesting than occasional glimpses of the river itself, which swelled after they left their own tributary. Tatiana shuddered, fearing if she had been forced to sail with the others, she would drown or at least become ill. Horses she could handle, having ridden since she was a child, and she tightened her grip on the reins each time they glimpsed the swiftly rushing water. To observe it from her tower reading room was one thing; getting too close was another entirely.

"You may continue for now to ride astride," Sir Mikhail said sternly when they had left their village and all sight of human habitation far behind. He frowned. "Your father was the one who permitted the use of those groomsman's breeches. For now. We permit them, as well, yet only so we can travel at a speedier pace."

Dimitri grinned, and Tatiana tried not to smile back. It was a sweet victory.

Nights the quartet usually made camp along the sandy shoreline, and so after several days she became accustomed to the river's rapid flow and its unceasing roar. Based on the maps she and Sonya had studied beforehand, she knew the remainder of her party would arrive long before she and the knights. The others would dock soon after this river converged with the legendary Volga. Still, Tatiana did not envy them.

The knights spoke to their lady seldom, and she had no objection to the silence—or their cooking. Each morning Sir

Igor would ride ahead with his bow and arrow, returning by the time they stopped for the evening with a string of rabbits, squirrels, and opossums to roast over the fire. Turnips, beets, cabbages, and apples from the previous summer's crops supplemented their meat.

Sir Dimitri, youngest of the three—and the only one whose brown beard had not yet turned grey (like Igor's) or white (like Mikhail's)—kept his mount close to hers all day. Fortunately, they encountered nothing and no one that presented a danger, including the feared bears, wolves, and especially boars. Yet Tatiana remained nervous as they rounded each riverbend, often forgetting to keep her eyes on the tall fur hats of the riders ahead of her.

Days passed. Then a week. Then two. Eventually she slept more soundly on the dirt and gravel. Her buttocks and thighs stopped aching at the end of each day. Not only did she grow accustomed to full days in the saddle, but to frequent bouts of needle-like rain, incessant drizzle, and dense fog.

At times she bantered with the knights, which they seemed to appreciate. Around the fire the men shared tales of battles, as well as relived the marvels of cities to which they had traveled. Dimitri especially enjoyed sharing descriptions of Moskva and its architectural spectacles. His accounts were so vivid she could almost imagine the capital.

"Will there be chances to explore the forest?" she asked once.

"*Oy!* Not a remote one," Igor insisted.

"Why not? Do they not have forests around the capital?"

"They do. Unsafe ones," Mikhail pronounced firmly.

"So how do people hunt? Or search for wood?"

"The forests are filled with marauders and brigands," Dimitri explained. "No one dares to enter unless totally armed. Only a few of the tsar's huntsmen make use of it."

"As for wood," Mikhail added, pointing to the log he was about to toss on the fire, "these are as valuable as gold bars in Moskva."

"Trust me," Dimitri said seriously. "The forests outside the palace and the squares are no place for innocent people, and especially not children or women."

Disappointed, Tatiana went back to asking questions about the markets and palaces and visitors, all of which the three seemed eager to discuss. "You will see little of that, though," Mikhail responded one evening, curtly dismissing her questions. "Ladies do not wander on their own."

"Certainly not without a male escort," Igor added.

We'll see, Tatiana thought.

At times the four encountered small outposts, as well as post stations that offered meager provisions and fresh horses if needed. They'd long since left Tolkov territory, and Tatiana noticed that the knights seemed less relaxed and more attentive to their surroundings. When possible they secured an actual featherbed mattress for their lady, as well as a warm and dry room with a single gigantic stove. Most times, however, she continued to settle for a hard dirt floor outside while the knights alternated keeping watch for wild animals or robbers.

It occurred to her one evening as she lay on her cloak trying to identify star constellations that by now she must have passed her birthday. She would have turned ten and eight years old—without fanfare or the party her father usually held in her honor. This should have made her happy, though the bogatyrs seemed oblivious. However, it meant that sooner rather than later, her excuses for not being married would sound thinner.

Since midsummer had arrived, the paths between outposts grew busier, and the men correspondingly more vigilant. "With so many eligible women enroute to Moskva, this is double the usual traffic," Dimitri commented as more and more horses, wagons, and walkers thickened the bumpy, muddy route.

"When will we arrive in Yaroslavl?"

"Tomorrow. Then you will see wonders that will make you happy you are on this journey." He spoke lightly with a reassuring smile, as if he knew how much she resented having to be here. Wonders or not, she had had no desire to leave the castle for such a long period. She swallowed hard and rode ahead of a protesting Mikhail to catch up with a young lady ahead. The girl—and she was hardly more than that—was one of the few besides Tatiana riding astride her own mount. Most of the contestants, as she now thought of the hapless women summoned against their will to Moskva, rode double behind a man, side-saddle, or trapped inside a rickety wagon that could barely get down the well-worn, often nearly impassable paths.

The girl, just as others Tatiana had encountered at a few post stations thus far, did not wish to converse. After a couple failed attempts, Tatiana shrugged this off as a result of her men's attire, which she stubbornly continued to wear. She dropped back then to face Mikhail's wrath.

"It is not safe for you to leave us and ride ahead!" he chided, throwing an angry look at Dimitri, who must take the blame.

"Nothing is safe, is it?" she shot back, resenting her perceived loss of freedom. "Why even live?"

"You have no idea, My Lady," Mikhail said, and she knew she'd sounded ungrateful, not to mention risked an end to all the progress she had made bonding with the knights.

Igor had ridden ahead to prepare places for them to stay in the capital, and now she sensed Mikhail and Dimitri riding closer to her than before.

Surrounded by creaking wheels, whinnying horses, screaming children, and cracking whips for hours on end, Tatiana developed a headache that made jostling on a horse all day persistently unpleasant. What lay ahead of her, she did not wish to consider.

***

Dressed for the first time in weeks in a flowing woman's sarafan (at Mikhail's insistence and to Dimitri's bemusement), Tatiana could only gape at the distant horizon.

That horizon soon transformed itself into something she never could've imagined: an endless row of cathedrals and monasteries, spread out in a long strand like shimmering gems on a river necklace. Dozens of clusters of gold and silver cupolas, as well as green and blue enamel turrets and towers sprinkled with stars, rose from each cathedral like bubbles drifting heavenward. There were so many elaborately carved wooden churches—perhaps as many as a hundred—that Tatiana wondered if there were enough saints to lend their names to each place of worship.

Grateful to have arrived safely with their lady, sirs Dimitri and Mikhail saw her settled in a tiny room in one of the stone monasteries before they went to pray. It appeared she would be left merely to imagine the magnificence of each iconostasis—the high tiers of bejeweled icons that most churches boasted and that divided worshippers from the clergy.

As soon as they had left, Tatiana shoved her hair up under a cap she had stolen from home, once again replaced her riding frock with breeches and a tunic, and strolled freely about the town as a young, still beardless lad. Now she could duck in and out of the magnificent churches, mingling with male worshippers and wizened old women with heads wrapped in floral-patterned scarves.

With the oblong coins she'd hidden in her pouch, she also sought out dumplings and apples from busy vendors who could barely stay upright amid all the foot and horse traffic. Settled near a fountain, she watched tradesmen, merchants, priests, farmers, knights, and a few old babushkas scurry about. It appeared that no young women had been released from their lodgings. Having grown up wandering at will through her village, she wondered at this, taking it as a discouraging harbinger of what might come when she reached the bigger capital city, Moskva.

Situated at the confluence of two rivers, Yaroslavl served as a crossroads for merchants from faraway countries. Their richly adorned costumes and pointed hats encircled with fur and gems were more impressive than the ones her own knights wore. Tatiana was enthralled by the pottery and metal workers, as well as brilliantly attired Tatars, Cossacks, and Russian nobles in silk, brocade, or cashmere kaftans plus matching red boots.

She spent the remainder of her coins on trinkets for her father and the servants left behind at the castle. Before dark she moved swiftly past a frowning priest who had no time to question a lackey entering the passageway. Slipping unseen into her assigned room, she felt a sense of satisfaction at her escapade. For the first time on the journey, she had enjoyed an entire day, observing to herself that she might like travel after all.

In the morning they were reunited with the rest of their party, and Olga, Sonya, and Masha talked incessantly from the moment they saw her. Everyone seemed to have survived the trip unscathed. Soon they boarded a flat barge that would transport everyone downriver to a place where they could disembark for the final portion of their voyage to the capital. Tatiana overcame her nervousness to walk aboard bravely, keeping a tight grip on the holding ropes that would protect the passengers as well as restrain the terrified horses during the passage.

Mother Volga, as they called the massive river that dissected the countryside and the territory of Rus, appeared to be a woman of multiple moods who danced according to the sunlight or cloud patterns. Tatiana's favorite was the western sunset, its colors reflected in a watery tapestry over the waves and the wake, surpassing anything she could recall. She made her way to the rear of the boat and nudged aside one of the horses to admire cherry and orange cloud swirls against an opalescent sky. Surely this alone was worth all the weeks hunched over her horse's saddle. She forgot to be afraid and fell asleep on a rough blanket on deck.

Soon enough they docked, and now they would use a wagon to transport her, Olga, Sonya, and Masha. Tatiana resented the new restriction, realizing how much she missed the freedom of her horse's movements and, miraculously, the smooth sailing of the boat. The wagon jostled every bit of her body, and at first the incessant chattering of her female companions grinded on her nerves.

Until now, it had been easy enough to ignore the real purpose of her journey. However, the ladies had spent a long time in Yaroslavl. There they'd gleaned tidbits of gossip, innuendo, and some useful information about this pilgrimage being made simultaneously by all the noble women within a forty-day ride of the tsar's palace.

"I'm afraid all the scholarly knowledge I've given you will not help you earn the tsarevich's hand in marriage," Sonya told her. "From what I can determine, most of these ladies are unschooled. The contest will revolve solely around beauty."

"I don't care," Tatiana shrugged. She had no expectation of winning, and certainly no desire to marry a prince—or anyone—and leave her home.

"My lady will have an excellent chance then," Olga said to the others. "Just look at her beauty!"

"Ridiculous. I am not beautiful."

"You are," Olga and Masha protested in unison.

Perhaps she was. Her mirror at the castle told her so, as did most of the villagers and of course her father. She knew she had strong yet soft features, deep green eyes, and luscious long reddish hair that looked lovely when she had it combed out and Olga had removed all the bits and pieces of grass and leaves. Not lovely enough, most assuredly, to compete against what would surely be hundreds or potentially thousands of other women? "Ridiculous," she repeated.

"You must be careful," Masha said, looking around as if worried someone would overhear them even over the noise of the wagon. "Wait a bit," she urged when Tatiana gave her a questioning look.

When they stopped for a meal, Masha stirred stew in a large pot over the fire they shared with another small group. "Above all," she whispered loudly, "you must be cognizant of what you eat! From now on only I will be permitted to prepare your food unless you must attend a banquet."

"So that I do not get too plump for his highness?"

"No, to ensure you don't get poisoned!" Olga almost hissed. Trust it to her lady's maid to be so overprotective.

Poisoned? "By whom? And why? Why would you say such a thing?" she asked with a touch of amusement in her voice.

"My Lady, it has happened in the past," Sonya explained. She motioned Olga and Tatiana to a log where they settled their long skirts so they could eat. "It is an historical fact that previous ladies who competed for the crown have been poisoned—or at least drugged."

"Tell us," Tatiana demanded, completely flabbergasted by this news. For a moment, she recalled the vial of poison antidote that Baba had given her.

"Always," Sonya continued, "this type of competition has aroused hatred and subterfuge. The chronicles report that when Tsar Michael ruled, both his fiancée and then his first wife succumbed! They had a bride show then, as well."

"I heard the same," Olga added. "They say both were poisoned or drugged. Regardless of which, both went mad."

Sonya went on to relate how a later prince's chosen bride fared: "He was madly in love with his first choice until her jealous ladies twisted her golden hair so tightly she fainted."

"And then what?"

"The court physicians pronounced it epilepsy before exiling her to Siber. That is when he selected his second choice. Alas, she died young after giving him only baby girls. There were many families, you see, vying for influence and the throne. Now, too, they will all want their representative to win the contest."

Tatiana shot a somewhat angry look at her tutor. "Why, pray tell, did I not know about this *before* we left home?"

Sonya opened and closed her mouth helplessly but did not reply.

"Hmm," Tatiana mused a short time later. "Perhaps some of the women prayed *not* to be chosen. I know I would—I will," she added. "After all, it sounds like a high stakes game, with that much interfering and plotting. Yet do you believe that could happen *now*?"

"I pray not, My Lady," Sonya replied, and then helped her up as Mikhail motioned them back to the wagon.

"We will light candles for you!" Masha added.

I hope, Tatiana prayed, *that I am not a serious contender.* Not even choice number fifty!

Chapter 6

Just after sunrise they entered Moskva, capital of both the principality of Muscovy and the vast tsardom of Rus.

At the outskirts, Sir Igor rejoined them and advised against any delay. "We must hurry and get the women settled. By sunset it will not be safe to remain outdoors," he warned.

"Why not?" Masha asked.

"Marauders with axes and cudgels roam the streets."

"Axes?" Masha said fearfully.

Tatiana shivered the way she hadn't when she'd first heard these dire warnings. She felt Dimitri's horse narrow the gap between them. She was now permitted to ride again, albeit side-saddle.

Unable to hear anyone else, Tatiana let go of the saddle to cover her ears against the cacophony of bells that pealed louder and louder as they passed the Moskva River. Along its placid banks, peddlers, jewelers, pushcart men, and laundry women availed themselves of the filthy water.

Dimitri laughed at her. "I neglected to warn you that there are forty times forty churches here, and each one rings its bells all day and night."

Truly, the bells seemed to vibrate in waves across the city, and Tatiana knew she would never get accustomed to such an ear-splitting clash of melodies.

Approaching the red- and white-walled Kremlin broken up by twenty brick towers (each topped by a set of archers and pikemen perched in perpetual readiness), Tatiana nearly tumbled from her mare. The sight of the churches rising from within dazzled the senses. Above them dozens of golden cupolas topped with nipple-like crosses reached for the sky.

She barely noticed the muddy roads and tiny log huts stuffed with moss and hugging the Kremlin walls. It was all she could do to keep up with Sir Igor as he led them inside an elaborate palace and then stood outside the entryway to what appeared to be a small hall.

"The ladies will stay here," he pronounced. "I will stable the horses and guard the wagon and our supplies."

It turns out she and her ladies were to sleep on cushioned mats in this room occupied by over a dozen other contenders and their ladies. This was not at all what she had envisioned, and Sonya frowned as she searched for a place for a servant to set down the large worn trunk that held all Tatiana's gowns.

Because they had traveled so far, it was only days before

the balls would begin, leaving no free time—if there were such a thing here—to explore Moskva. It became immediately apparent that each group of ladies would be expected to remain sequestered in one of these quarters, known as terems, until commanded to appear at the bride show.

Sonya and Masha, on the other hand, enjoyed some liberty to roam, and abruptly left to wander the palace and make friends of their counterparts. Sonya, her services as tutor not needed except to instruct her charge in royal decorum, had taken the younger cook under her wings.

"We will learn what we can about the competition rules," Sonya assured her lady before they left. "And before dinner Masha will determine what she can from the maids of the other contenders."

Sighing, Tatiana agreed to this arrangement, and she and Olga settled on their pallets for a much-needed rest. Now that she was here, she was too weary to protest, as if it would do her any good anyway. After weeks of rough travel, she fell into a sound sleep with Olga sitting up as her guard in case anyone tried to steal their goods—or worse, harm Lady Tolkov.

"It is a most fierce competition," Masha whispered urgently later that evening. She had brought fresh bread, blackberries, and wine with her, which Tatiana ate happily.

"Fierce in what way? You mean the way we discussed?'

Masha looked meaningfully at Sonya, who moved closer. "No, I just mean that there will be four balls, preceded by banquets. Each night dozens if not a hundred ladies will be eliminated."

"Eliminated?" For a moment Tatiana imagined the worst.

"Cut from the competition," Sonya clarified. "The ministers and nobles—the boyars—will ask them to depart the following morning. Only a select few from each ball will remain."

"And then?"

"The fourth ball will be for the finalists only."

"So we may be permitted to head home as soon as the end of this week?"

"Yes, My Lady. At the latest after the third or fourth ball," Masha assured her.

When two of the tsar's counselors showed up in the morning to examine each woman, Tatiana balked.

"I am not a hog at the market!" she protested as she watched others ahead of her undergo the beginnings of a physical exam in a small antechamber.

Each woman or girl—for some were barely of marriageable age—underwent a thorough examination of feet, teeth, ears, mouth, hip bones, and even breasts. "They must ensure there are no men in disguise," Olga, who had been permitted to stay with her for the ordeal, whispered. "Also, the chosen lady must be fit to bear children."

When it was Tatiana's turn, she submitted with a lack of grace. No one had handled her thus in her entire life, and certainly no man had ever taken such liberties as to tug at her braid to ensure her hair was real. The ultimate insult seemed to be when one of the doctors pinched her breast through her coat! Then she nearly bit the man who stuck his grimy hands into her mouth and tugged at her teeth.

However, the worst was yet to come. The court physician dragged her by her braid and forced her struggling onto a cot she hadn't seen previously. Here his assistant and a midwife spread her legs apart before the physician poked something bulky up inside her!

Appalled, she had no idea what the doctor meant when, before releasing her, he said loudly, "Hymen intact!"

She scrambled off the cot and raced out of the room. *Why had no one warned her?*

"Night three," the scribe with a checklist pronounced behind her, thus sentencing her to wait inside the women's quarters for three entire days and nights.

"You must be a virgin to compete," Olga explained when she re-entered the women's chamber in tears.

"I have never lain with a man! I have never even been kissed!"

"They cannot merely accept your word," Olga said soothingly. "You do know what happens between a man and a woman, do you not?"

Tatiana flushed. She had watched animals in the forest and horses in the stables. Yes, she knew. Somehow until now it hadn't occurred to her that her own future children would come out of such an act. She would not think about it until she had to!

Alas, there was little to keep her mind occupied except admiring the elaborate satin, brocade, and silk gowns of the other contestants. Most devoted their time to embroidering incredible designs on their collars, sleeves, aprons, and hats. Since Tatiana detested this most womanly of pursuits, she happily turned over the bulk of the tasks to Olga. Could life get any more tedious than this?

She also tried passing time by striking up conversations with some of the other contenders. Sadly, more often than not such overtures met with rebuffs from the ladies or their female relatives. She did not consider herself so attractive that she would pose a threat, and at first was puzzled. Only after careful observation did she realize that many of the would-be brides seemed terrified rather than jealous. Tatiana initially had assumed each desperately wanted to win the bridal competition; now it did not seem so.

When she voiced her thoughts to Olga and Sonya, they confirmed her suspicions.

"Some will be punished horribly by their families if they don't win," Olga murmured.

"The rest fear imprisonment for the remainder of their lives," Sonya added. "The imperial women are sequestered for life in this kind of a terem except for when ordered to report to his majesty's or his highness's bed chamber. Of course, the royal terem is much more luxurious and much larger."

"It is also a dangerous position, that of tsaritsa, or wife of the tsar. As wife of the tsarevich, the winner will be equally at risk," Olga whispered. "After all, no one knows *exactly* how this prince's first wife died last year, and many women fear they may meet their deaths the same way."

Tatiana shuddered. She wanted nothing more than to travel back to her father and their castle, even if it meant never marrying at all. Which she hoped it did!

Yet before she returned home, she longed to see more of Moskva and the wonders Dimitri and the others had described. It seemed patently unfair that only men and female servants or old women were permitted to venture out. Thus, since she would not be missed for the next couple days, Tatiana determined to escape what she now considered her prison. The odds of returning here in her lifetime were negligible.

There was one main problem: a trio of guards stationed outside the huge room. Only maidservants, young boys, and those balancing platters of food and bottles of wine were permitted to enter and exit the terem.

By day two, she realized some women and their female escorts were permitted to leave to pray in a chapel. Suddenly she felt herself overcome by a spell of piety.

While a reluctant Sonya held up a cloth to shield her, Tatiana slipped her boy's clothing under her frock and then her cloak. If there was a way to escape via the chapel, she wanted to be prepared. She hid the servant's cap she would need to tie up her reddish-gold hair in a pouch.

"I'm doing this for educational purposes," she whispered firmly to her tutor. She had told no one about her similar disguise in Yaroslavl.

"I don't want to know anything!" Sonya said, looking away. For a moment the two stared at one another, and Tatiana feared Sonya might report her before she could escape. But the older woman's gaze softened, and Tatiana relaxed.

The plan worked much easier than she'd imagined. Grabbing Masha's arm to tug her out of the church without giving her a chance to protest, Tatiana managed to slip out the door in the square surrounded by other cathedrals. Masha, her linen shirt hidden by an unadorned and somewhat shabby long-sleeved, plain sarafan and her hair beneath a veil as befitting a female servant shopping for her master, attracted no attention. Nor did the "boy" at her side, who, after removing her long women's cloak in a shadowed alley, wore a similar linen shirt covered by a belted tunic that reached past her knees. The hat over her upswept hair completed her ensemble.

Once she had convinced—or actually threatened—Masha to keep her thoughts to herself and not reveal anything, Tatiana led their way down the hill leading away from one of the churches. From there they emerged into a bustling marketplace in a second square outside the kremlin.

At the southeast end of what Masha told her was Trinity Square, called Krasnaya (Red) or Beautiful Square by some, they immediately beheld an amazing sight—an architectural confection! From what Dimitri had told her one night by the fire, she supposed it must be the Trinity Sobor, or Cathedral, which some people referred to by the name of Saint Basil's. "Tsar Ivan the Fourth ordered it built to commemorate a great victory along the Volga," Dimitri had explained. "Legend has it that the architects had their eyes cut out afterward to ensure they would never be able to duplicate such a marvel."

"It's breathtaking!" she exclaimed now to Masha.

"It is indeed, My Lady,"

"Shush. I am just Tanya."

"Yes, My—Tanya. Did you want to pray inside? Only," she hastened to add, "if it is the proper time."

"Of course it is." Tatiana knew well that women having their monthly bleeding were prohibited from entering a church. Fortunately, she had suffered hers while traveling with the knights, none of them the wiser due to the pile of torn cloths in her saddle bag.

Before praying, however, she wanted to huddle in an out-of-the-way corner to drink in the sight while she could. The sobor presented a visual medley of cupolas, decorated archways, striped and golden cupolas, and brilliant colors on a red and white brick background. The entire ensemble of nine magnificent smaller chapels surrounding one extremely tall one resembled the gold-tipped flames of a giant bonfire rising toward heaven. She had never seen anything so magnificent, even in Yaroslavl.

After leaving behind the elaborately decorated frescoes inside one of the chapels, Tatiana and Masha meandered the square, trying not to stand anywhere and gawk lest they draw attention to themselves. Two shops were busily engaged in hollowing out various sized logs with an ax. "Coffins," Masha whispered.

Barbers occupied an entire row of other shops. Since nearly all males in Rus wore beards, mustaches, and shoulder length hair, these men were the busiest. Rather than letting the snippings pile up, however, young boys scooped them in their hats and wandered around the rain-soaked ground strewing the clippings between logs to shore up the muddy square.

Without a midday meal, the two young women delighted in spending Tatiana's coins on meat pies, raspberries, and slices of watermelon sold by vendors with trays roped around their necks or by produce sellers with baskets full of luscious fruits and vegetables. Other vendors busied themselves creating the gingerbread, sugary pastries, candies, jellies, and breads they had baked in various shapes.

Delighting in the square's constant activity and in the disguise that brought her freedom, Tatiana spent the remainder of the afternoon shopping for amber earrings and watching jugglers, bear tricks, acrobats, and musicians. For a while they observed a portable puppet theater show.

"We must return," Masha urged.

Tatiana did so reluctantly. Then she discovered her women's clothing had been stolen from its hiding place! Since she had just watched nearly naked men in the square's taverns selling the threads from their own clothing to buy beer in the numerous taverns, she was unsurprised.

When Masha returned with a long coat to slip over her lady's head, Tatiana heaved a sigh. She knew she had just experienced something and someplace that would have to last her a lifetime. Exactly what that life would bring, however, she had no idea.

Back in the terem glancing at the twin insects trapped inside her new amber earrings, she felt as if nothing could equal this day.

Chapter 7

The crowded terem thinned quickly after the first and second balls. Most young women looked relieved to depart, even if their mothers sometimes pulled their ears while escorting them out. Only a few remaining ones looked excited that they would get an opportunity to continue to the next round of the bride show.

Tatiana, Olga, and Sonya spent afternoons and early evenings hunched over Tatiana's dresses and robes, embroidering them with butterflies and peacocks (her idea), dragonflies (Sonya's idea), and coins (Olga's idea). They stitched with colored, silver, and gold threads, then sewed on dozens of pearls, metal beads, and gemstones. Lord Nicholas had sent along a pouch full of stones with Dimitri, who had entrusted the jewels to Sonya to bring into the terem.

Arguments swirled about them, mostly between mothers and daughters. The latter often dissolved into tears. For the first time in years, Tatiana felt almost relieved not to have a mother to order her around, the way the other young ladies did. This way she could overrule her ladies, including the opinionated Olga, on choices of garments.

She also relished the silence that descended each afternoon as everyone stretched out for the obligatory nap. It was then she could dream about everything she had seen and done thus far. She imagined the banquet and ball that had to occur before she could go home. Hopefully sirs Dimitri, Mikhail, and Igor would not wish to stay in Muscovy through the winter. Already the terem's stuffiness made her sweat, so she suspected the harsh Russian winters would be much more unpleasant here in these drafty accommodations than in her cozy room at Tolkov Castle.

For her first and hopefully only banquet, she decided to wear a silver brocade robe with an underskirt of white taffeta embroidered with silver beads and pearls. The open robe trimmed with gold thread glistened, as did the smattering of diamonds on its shoulders and around the hem. A high fur collar decorated with emeralds and rubies added color, as did the black freshwater pearls that adorned her silver *kokoshnik* or headdress. A gauzy silver veil offered only a tantalizing look at her eyes. Plenty of thin mica or silver plates that served as mirrors assured her she could compete with the best of the brilliantly gowned women around her. If she had wanted to compete, that is.

About a hundred women and their mothers or escorts now lined up to be paraded into the massive, gilded dining hall, illuminated by thousands of candles and graced with elegant wall tapestries. The meal would last for four hours under intense scrutiny by royal councilors, observers, and boyars. Since Tatiana had no mother, Sonya was permitted to escort her, having dressed in a modest silk gown the color of a goldfinch and a matching *kokoshnik* decorated with orange citrine and white pearls.

Tatiana sipped and munched delicately, her stomach beginning to churn. None of this had seemed real until she was in the midst of the competition, and suddenly she was acutely aware of so many eyes scrutinizing her. Sometimes a counselor would tap a young woman or her mother on the shoulder, and the two would shuffle out of the hall in disgrace. Perhaps, Tatiana observed, their table manners had eliminated them, and for a few minutes she considered letting her food drool down the front of her gorgeous ensemble.

She was only vaguely aware of the literally dozens of courses set in front of her. She'd partaken of little more than tea and melon earlier that day, yet could barely ingest more than a few bites of the rich dishes: roasted meats, creatively decorated fowl, open-mouthed fish, and thick cream soups. She half hoped someone would tap her on the shoulder and usher her back to the terem where she could pack for home. Only gentle reminders from Sonya kept her spearing her gold utensils into an occasional piece of pork or pheasant.

Tatiana knew that plumpness was considered desirable in the tsardom's women, so she resolved to try a bit harder for form's sake. Yet all her strolls in her father's castle halls and in the forest had kept her leaner than the desired weight. Fortunately, she did not care.

Apparently neither the tsar nor his son the tsarevich took part in the banquets, which appeared to be nothing more than a test of the decorum and table manners for the contestants. "Only the tsar will attend the ball later," Sonya mentioned quietly. "The tsarevich will not appear until the final ball tomorrow when the dancing part of the show ends and more eliminations have been made."

Relieved, albeit somewhat nervous about dancing in front of the tsar, Tatiana now decided that at least she should do her father proud. Being sent home *too* early in disgrace might offend her companions and the villagers of Tolkov, as well.

At long last the women took turns entering a huge ballroom magnificently decorated with gilded panels, statues, masses of cut flowers, and chandeliers with so many candles they appeared to threaten a dozen lives below them if they fell. As each woman entered, a red robed crier announced her name, village or city, and rank, if she had one.

"Lady Tatiana Nicholaevna of Tolkov Castle!" she heard, dropping her best curtsy in the direction of the richly gowned man perched on a bejeweled throne at the end of the hall. Behind the tsar—for this surely must be he—stood two boyars or nobles dressed in ankle-length white velvet kaftans and matching fox fur hats towering above their already enormous height.

Tatiana took her place in one of two facing lines. The ballroom easily accommodated the more than one thousand people gracing it, and between the decorations and the costumes, she felt as if she were living inside one of the fairytales she'd read.

Knights and noblemen had been enlisted as dancing partners. For a moment Tatiana felt as if she could not recall a single step. Only when the orchestra music rose to a crescendo and the man across from her bowed did she recall what she was supposed to do.

She was, she knew, not by any means the most graceful dancer in the room. The best she could do was follow the knight's lead and try to stay off his toes from dance to dance.

This became slightly more difficult as she could no longer blend in so inconspicuously once the judges began to tap arms and shoulders to motion dancers to leave the floor.

Now each of the remaining women would line up in front of the tsar, who sat resplendent in gold and wearing a sable collar and matching crown. Each lady was asked to pronounce her name while sinking into another deep curtsy. Tatiana barely registered the man with a quill making check marks on a piece of parchment.

From what she could tell, she had advanced to the final round. Like it or not.

***

Tatiana slept late the final morning, leaving it to her ladies to prepare her apparel. She simply wanted this to end.

As she nibbled grapes and oranges from the ever-replenished platters, she knew no one could poison her without doing the same to the other remaining contenders. Some women, she could tell, looked terrified, while others seemed excited. Her own feelings ran somewhere down the middle.

Sonya, Olga, and Masha arranged for her to wash in a

small hipbath before painting scarlet color on her cheeks and darkening her eyebrows. Fighting with her maid to get her way, Tatiana declined the usual thick makeup and power that other young women favored. Olga did, however, brush out her hair until its reddish-gold highlights gleamed. Rather than wear it in a braid like most unmarried women, she had insisted on taking the risk of leaving it loose. Perhaps, she hoped, this alone might disqualify her.

These preparations occupied most of the day, interspersed by the afternoon nap, yet all too soon it was time to dress.

Tonight she would wear a royal blue robe and underskirt bordered with gold braid and embroidered with peacocks on both sides. Tiny butterflies danced down each of the long sleeves. All of the peacock eyes and feathers were further adorned with sapphires, emeralds, and diamonds, matched by those dangling from her ears and bedecking her fingers. Masha draped a gold lace veil over the tall sky-blue *kokoshnik* garlanded in ropes of pearls that towered above her hair and also covered her forehead.

She admired the headdress, wondering idly for the first time if the tsarevich were taller than she. Perhaps at least her dancing partner would be. Might one of her father's cousins be invited tonight? It would be more fun to dance with some- one she knew.

"When will we see the little grand duchess?" she thought to ask while Olga reattached two pearls that had fallen off. No one had mentioned Snowdrop since their arrival and the girl had not attended last night's banquet or ball. "Is she too young to attend?"

"I presume she is in her private terem," Olga said quietly.

"They say she has her own pets, waterfalls, and dining quarters."

For some reason Masha looked uncomfortable and changed the subject to the emerald silk slippers her mistress would wear.

Tatiana tried again. "Surely tonight she would want to be present to see her future stepmother. I know I would want to if my father staged such a competition to find a new bride."

Still no one responded. Tatiana briefly recalled the villagers' odd behavior whenever the girl was mentioned, yet she promptly dismissed Snow from her mind.

***

The banquet seemed to go much quicker this time, with the chattering enlivening the room coming mostly from ambassadors, high ranking officials, and contestants' mothers. The entrants themselves seemed too nervous to eat or chat. Tatiana felt the same.

Way down her assigned table she spotted Dimitri and Mikhail, both engaged in conversation with two elaborately gowned older women across from them. Once Mikhail smiled encouragingly in her direction, and she smiled back nervously.

By the time the banquet ended and the noise faded, one by one the ladies under contention rose and moved toward the adjoining ballroom. There they formed a circle and began a slow parade around the huge room. Each stopped at the appropriate place to drop a deep curtsy.

Her eyes cast down demurely, Tatiana did not realize until

she approached the tsar that tonight there were three thrones. Surely the handsome man wearing a crown on the left, who appeared to be in his mid thirties, must be Tsarevich or Prince Alexander. She had expected him to be much older, as the tsar himself appeared elderly. Instead, the prince's eyes seemed to twinkle with youth. Each lady was to curtsy three times, and only after she had done so in front of the tsar did Tatiana realize that the middle throne was occupied by a girl of about twelve wearing a gold circlet on her pale blond hair.

This, then, must be the Grand Duchess Snowdrop, so often referred to by the same title her mother had held: princess, or tsarevna. Somehow Tatiana had envisioned her as a small child who might be eager for a new mother. Yet the look on the princess's face was as hard and tight as that of a much older person, and she did not smile at either Tatiana or the lady ahead of her. In fact, her eyes seemed to glow from a distance with an almost reddish cast. Nonetheless, Tatiana gave a wan smile and continued her curtsies.

A uniformed official stationed himself behind the tsarevich and the princess, hastily scribbling notes. Occasionally Alexander would look up at him and say something no one could hear.

Tatiana moved on. Someone took her hand and led her onto the dance area. She didn't care who it was. Snow's fiery eyes had disconcerted her; on the other hand, Prince Alexander's own eyes had seemed warm and admiring in that briefest of moments she looked at him.

She forgot both of them when she saw it was Sir Dimitri who was to escort her into her first dance. "I hope you don't mind, My Lady. I asked for the privilege of dancing with you."

"It's fine. More than fine, kind sir," she added, suddenly feeling at ease to be in Dimitri's arms for one of the few dances that involved touching. Tonight he looked more splendid than ever, his floor-length forest green coat with gold buttons a perfect contrast to her blues.

They spoke little, until Tatiana confessed to him all about her forbidden visit into Moskva. "It is the only time I've felt enjoyment on this trip," she defended herself before he could protest. No need to admit to the Yaroslavl deception, as well.

Rather than scold her, he threw back his head and laughed. It was a wonderful sound, and although she felt relieved that he did not chastise her, she also felt a sense of warmth and bonding with her cousin and own castle's knight.

"Only you, My Lady Tatiana, could think up such a thing."

"Is that a criticism or a compliment?"

"Definitely the latter. You are a credit to your position—albeit some would say not so much to your gender."

She smiled up at him. "I miss my father," she said suddenly.

"You two are close."

"We are. And this winter I nearly lost him!"

"I heard about that when we returned. Thank God he survived."

For a moment she was tempted to tell him about Baba Yaga. Yet before she could make that decision, someone approached them.

"His Imperial Highness would claim this next dance," the man said.

It was time, then. She was happy now, and definitely not ready to leave someone familiar.

"Of course," Dimitri conceded. Before releasing her, he leaned over and whispered: "We all agree he would be a fool *not* to choose you."

Flushed and grateful for the encouragement, she could merely nod and permit herself to be led away toward the thrones where the prince stood.

With a kind smile, Tsarevich Alexander reached out his arms, which she went toward nervously. What would they talk about? How much was she expected to say? How long might this dance last?

As they moved into the center of the hall, Tatiana was aware of all the looks following them. Curious ones. Angry ones. Approving ones. Jealous ones. Already she noted that the ballroom's corners seemed occupied by dozens of furious and resentful girls who had been shuffled over there until they hopefully would be chosen as someone's partner.

"My Lady Tatiana," the prince said as the music that had temporarily stopped now started up again with a melodious waltz. She prayed she could keep herself from stomping on his royal highness's boots.

"You look astonishing," he said after twirling her on yet a third dance. She could smell his breath, a sweet combination of lavender and mint.

"Thank you, Your Imperial Highness."

"Please call me Alexander."

"Yes, Your—Alexander. And please call me Tanya."

"You are an excellent seamstress, Tanya" he commented. "I've never seen such exquisitely crafted apparel."

Knowing full well that a lack of sewing talent might disqualify her, she admitted the truth. "I am nothing but thumbs when I touch a needle. It is my ladies who deserve all the credit. I merely made suggestions."

"Ah. I confess the butterflies are my favorite. We have all colors and species in the surrounding forests."

"I thought the forest was a dangerous, forbidden place?"

"True, although not when you bring your own army along," he laughed.

When the music stopped again, he bowed as she curtsied, fully expecting him to move on to the next lady awaiting her turn. Surprisingly, he asked, "May I have this next dance as well?"

She wasn't certain whether she was more surprised or flattered. Surely the two dozen or so remaining ladies could not all have had their turns yet. As she glanced about the room, however, she noticed that their number continued to shrink dramatically.

She and the tsarevich continued their discussion about the forest, and she confided how much she enjoyed spending time there. He seemed genuinely interested, asking her intelligent questions about birds and trees until she nearly forgot who he was. Forgot, that is, until she caught a glimpse of Snowdrop's disapproving gaze.

"I must dance elsewhere now," he said with what sounded like a trace of reluctance. Of course, he must move around. And why would a royal personage with hair that glowed the shade of autumn wheat just before sunset care about her with all these elegant women around? She hoped, however, to get at least one more chance to gaze into those brown eyes with a hint of jasper coloring them.

Sensing another gentleman moving swiftly in her direction, Tatiana made a quick shuffle toward a giant pewter punchbowl to avoid gaining a new dance partner. Thus she was standing close enough now to hear the tsar speaking with his granddaughter.

The girl glanced over at Tatiana, and then, as if deliberately, she raised her voice to the man scribbling notes and said distinctly, "*Not* the ugly skinny one with the boorish peacock dress, please!"

Embarrassed and humiliated, Tatiana drained her punch and moved toward the exit, only to find her way blocked by two guards.

"I must get some air," she said, fanning herself with her hands.

"Not without an escort."

The second man said more sternly, "Not until the ball is pronounced finished and the royal family departs."

Fortunately, she now spied a few stools along one wall and hurried to claim one.

Was she really that ugly? Was the dress? Or was the princess—the Grand Duchess Snowdrop—just a spoiled child?

Chapter 8

I knew it! She's the most beautiful of all these women!" Masha cried enthusiastically that night after Sonya's announcement that Tatiana had been selected as one of five finalists.

"Shhh," Sonya made a hush motion. "Not everyone in here wants to hear such news. Our good news is their bad news."

Most of the terem had emptied of women, however, and supposedly so had the rest of the rooms that had harbored so many hopefuls for nearly a week. Tatiana imagined the reverse parade of travelers making a more somber horse and wagon exit from Moskva. Others would stay with their families for the royal wedding, as it was too far of a journey to return.

"You can tell us all about it in the morning," Sonya suggested, as if anyone would sleep soundly that night.

The decision to wait proved a wise one, since the remaining women and their mothers packed and left early in the morning when it was safe to travel. Fortunately, not a single one of the other four remaining contestants had been placed in this particular terem.

Before she could confide much of anything, however, they were interrupted by a bevy of servants scurrying in and out with trays of breads, cheeses, fruits, and juices more delightful than what had been served to them previously.

"Don't forget not to eat anything until we have sampled it," Masha barely had time to remind her.

Seamstresses and ladies followed close behind, each with an armful of gowns, sarafans with pleated long sleeves, soft linen blouses, and velvet or fur cloaks. Suddenly it seemed that Tatiana was expected to need a cosmetician, a hairdresser, three new ladies in waiting, and, astoundingly, her own jeweler.

Uncomfortable with all this attention, which also shunted her own women aside, she longed desperately for some privacy to continue relating to Olga, Sonya, and Masha what had transpired between her and the tsarevich the night before.

This was not to be, as the final contestants had been ordered to share tea with the tsarevich within a few hours.

The tsar, too, attended the tea, and as each girl bowed repeatedly before him, he dropped a gold and silver handkerchief sprinkled with pearls at their feet to show his pleasure. Only three women, however, were thus honored, and it was made clear that the other two would be sent home with wagonloads of gifts. The tsar had made his choices known; the final selection would be up to the groom.

Three women stood there trembling. Tatiana didn't know the other girls, only that they belonged to highly placed noble families. Sonya had explained that it would be preferable for the royal family to choose someone of the provincial gentry—like herself—rather than to forge more links to boyar factions who would be resented by their rivals if a girl from their house were chosen.

Regardless of the reason, Tatiana did not know whether she felt consternation or euphoria when the tsarevich reached out for her shaking hand and gently placed a gold and ruby ring on her finger!

She didn't know what happened to the other contenders, as the shock was too great for her to ponder the glamorous girls' fates. Presumably they would be dismissed with an array of gifts.

"Shall we stroll the gardens?" Alexander asked, and she could barely utter her assent.

Her "win" was shocking. Why would such a handsome royal personage care about her: a too slim, auburn-haired nobody from a second-rate noble house? A young woman, admittedly, with skin like honey and eyes that glowed the color of the palest sea, yet not someone who would cause anyone to take a second look. Yes, she had entered the dining hall today wearing a pearl-encrusted veil and bodice, as well as ruby-encrusted slippers that set off the pale rose of her silk gown, but was she really that special?

Tatiana stammered, blushed, curtsied profusely, and did all the typical things a shy young lady would do in the presence of an incredibly attractive young man who happened to be heir to the principality of Muscovy and the entire territory of Rus.

She let out her breath slowly. "Of course, Your Imperial Highness." He then guided her into a series of connected gardens, treating her as delicately as if she were one of the hand-blown glass doves used for table decorations. Indeed, her heart fluttered as fast as that of a frightened bird as she followed him.

Did she love him? Of course not. It was much too soon to know. Did she want to be his wife—anyone's wife? She long ago had decided the answer was negative. Yet she had no choice. She had been selected to wed him against all odds. What would happen if she refused?

That afternoon they did manage to talk and sometimes laugh as they strolled arm in arm past the peony gardens. And then the rose gardens. And then they inspected dozens of other royal gardens. Tatiana noticed little. She smelled none of the sweet floral scents, and gazed past the golden fountains and marble sculptures without noticing.

As he escorted her into a golden gazebo, he murmured, "Would you be my favorite wildflower, Tanya? My forever flower?"

She lost track of her surroundings. Could she do this? Must she do this? At least he *seemed* kind.

"Yes, I will," she murmured at last, but so quietly the tsarevich had to bend to hear her.

When he realized her answer, he waltzed her out of the gazebo, through the morning glory garden, and into the palace.

"I have found my new tsarevna and the future tsaritsa!" he announced to his attendants and anyone in sight.

By the time they'd crossed the last marble tiles leading into the palace, everyone had sensed or heard what had happened and came running. Royal butlers and royal cooks and royal seamstresses and royal footmen, all of whom had apparently been lurking in the shadows, now beamed with happiness.

"If you will permit me, Your Imperial Highness," interjected the royal steward, who suddenly emerged from a bench behind them. "I would like to welcome the Lady Tatiana to the tsardom of Rus. Long live Her Imperial Highness!"

Before he could finish, before the cooks could scurry to their posts to prepare a celebration meal, the sound of hoofbeats reverberated throughout the Kremlin. Led by the royal criers, uniformed horsemen dashed out of the courtyard and into the squares to spread the tidings throughout the kingdom. The people had waited for months and then these past days for the tsarevich to make his choice. Apparently, they were thrilled at the one he had made.

Tatiana was immensely flattered. And amazed. And somewhat dismayed. The idea of being royalty had not yet sunk in, let alone the fact that she might never be able to return to her father and her village.

Last night she had whispered to Olga the same burning question: "What happens if someone gets chosen and doesn't want to be?"

"She would have no choice," Olga whispered back. "You would have to have a serious flaw to escape the prince's choice."

Well, she didn't know what her flaws might be, except perhaps unwillingness and a streak of stubborness. She did feel confident of one thing, however: it might not be that difficult to learn to love this handsome, seemingly gentle man beside her—a man she had only known for fewer than three days.

This should have been the happiest day of her life. If only it were.

As the town bells pealed in all their noisy glory across the countryside, it appeared that it *was* a joyous day for everyone else. The entire Kremlin and indeed the city rejoiced. Only the soon-to-be bride had to paste a smile on her face.

Once, she raised her eyes to one of the Terem Palace's windows, where perhaps no one else noticed the pinched face framed with pale gold hair and half hidden behind one of the velvet curtains. If they had, the superstitious townspeople would have been truly terrified, for the face itself was so white it might have been that of a specter. And the eyes, glowing like embers that had rested too long on the fire, peered out long after the jubilant crowd had followed the prince and his bride-to-be inside.

***

Tatiana felt locked away for the days leading up to her wedding. Fortunately, this new terem was suitably larger, as befitting a royal. Yet there was no privacy, as a bevy of ladies in waiting, jesters, dwarfs, musicians, and servants consistently came and went. She had asked repeatedly about Sonya, Masha, and Olga, as well as Mikhail, Igor, and Dimitri. Nonetheless, no replies or explanations for their absence were forthcoming from anyone.

Nor was there a chance her father would get word and make it to Moskva on time. The tsar would tolerate no delay of his son's marriage, so within ten days the palace had organized the wedding. Since most of the kingdom's nobility had already gathered in one place for the balls, it seemed only prudent to keep them here for the other event. Most of the dukes and duchesses, barons and baronesses, and counts and countesses lived several days' journey on horseback, boat, and carriage. It wouldn't be fair to send them back to their castles, nor to make them incur the expense of returning a second time for the wedding. And most of the nobles met one another only once a year, if that, as the kingdom sprawled across a combination of hilly countryside, rain-drenched valleys, impassable rivers, thick forests, and arduous terrain.

The tsarevich, permitted to see her only occasionally and under heavy chaperone, asked her to call him Alex in private. It was obvious he looked forward to the big event much more than she did. "We will have fountains of champagne," he told her enthusiastically. "Rivers of chocolate. Mountains of mutton. I want everyone to feast until they feel one tenth as happy as I expect to be!"

"Alex," she protested, "it is costing so much."

"What else is gold for? What can be more precious or more worthwhile than my bride? And of course I can't wait for you to get acquainted with the other precious thing in my life. If she heard me call her a 'thing,' though, I'm afraid the foundations of the palace would rattle with her anger," he chuckled.

"Do you mean Snowdrop?"

He beamed. "Yes indeed, my other love, who I must admit I see far too little of."

Daily it dawned on her anew that the girl would be her own stepdaughter.

Perhaps it would be fun to have someone to be the younger sister she had never had. Or at least a companion. It did bother her, though, that after all this time, the two of them had not met.

True, Snowdrop had been ill during all except the last night of her father's inspection of the would-be brides. She had remained so throughout most of the courting, and purportedly was once again in the grips of some unspecified illness as the wedding approached. Alex assured his fiancée the girl would be well soon and that she looked forward to meeting Tatiana. So she dismissed her worries about Snowdrop's health, not to mention the nasty comments overheard at the ball about her stepmother-to-be. Tatiana struggled to imagine her as a younger version of her fiancé—and as exuberant as her father. Despite her misgivings, she could hardly wait to meet her officially.

One day before the wedding, Olga was permitted to visit the terem.

"We've all been thrilled for you! Worried, too, as no one from Tolkov has been allowed to see you. Are you well? Are you happy?"

"Slow down, please. One question at a time," she laughed. "And where have you been all this while?"

"We were advised that you would have your own ladies and staff from now forward, and until Sir Mikhail demanded in no uncertain terms that one of us gets to visit, it could not happen."

"And how are Mikhail and the other bogatyrs?"

"Rather grumpy, I would say. Dimitri sent Mikhail and Igor back to Tolkov to notify your father. He himself refuses to depart. I think he plans to attend the wedding. He is concerned about you and hopes I can assure him that you are well and happy."

"I am well, Olga. As for happiness, I cannot say. I must admit that I believe His Imperial Highness will make a good husband, though. Hopefully, that is."

"Thank God. Masha and Sonya wanted to stay in Moskva, as well. However, Igor and Mikhail said they must return home before winter sets in. They are permitted to stay here for now with Sir Dimitri, and send you their love and best wishes."

"And you managed to stay, as well?'

Olga sighed heavily, and Tatiana thought she looked older today than her thirty-two years.

"Is anything wrong? Should I speak to His Highness?"

"No, no. Nothing. I just think you should have someone you know—and trust—with you. Especially since you have no female relatives."

"I agree. If only my father were here. Though if you are making no progress with the woman who now dictates my life—her name is Countess Maria Tsergaya—I will speak to Alexander this afternoon. Perhaps he will listen."

The two women were hugging, both teary at a potential parting, when Countess Tsergaya entered the room to deliver another lecture on wedding protocol. "The tsar has informed me that this will be a joint wedding *and* coronation, so we have a dozen more rules to review."

After she had introduced the countess to her personal

maid and explained the situation, the countess looked Olga over coolly. "She may stay until after the coronation," she agreed. "But you must do as you are told," she warned Olga.

It was a great concession, Tatiana decided. Still, she vowed to speak with her prince and husband-to-be to persuade him that Olga should stay with her permanently. There was no reason to live so estranged from her one and only reminder of home.

Chapter 9

It was the grandest wedding anyone had seen in a lifetime, since the current tsar had never remarried after his second wife, who had died in childbirth thirty years ago. If this new bride seemed a bit subdued, no one noticed, particularly since the groom appeared content.

Tatiana tried her best to follow Countess Tsergaya's dictates, including a pre-wedding ritual cleansing in a banya. There a handful of ladies poured water on her and chanted sad songs that supposedly mourned the end of her life as a single girl. They also murmured what sounded like spells to ensure her husband would love her forever.

The bathing was followed by a lengthy combing of her hair, which must now be arranged into two braids, one signifying herself and the other her future offspring.

Backed up by Olga and her newly appointed ladies, Tatiana only argued once, and that was about her attire. "Brides may have worn red for centuries, yet I truly prefer gold," she insisted.

In the end they compromised, with the wedding gown consisting of a lace-trimmed blouse covered with a golden sarafan embroidered with swirls of red roses. Her neck rimmed with beads, jewels, and one huge ruby (a gift from Alex that matched her engagement ring) competed with the beauty of a high golden *kokoshnik*. A row of pearls masked her forehead, and a gold lace veil completed the ensemble.

On her wedding morning, Tatiana was led beneath a silver canopy from the stone Palace of Facets to the five-domed Italianate Assumption or Uspensky Cathedral on the Kremlin's north side. Here she was received by clergy members, the Archbishop of Moskva, and the Patriarch of Muscovy, who would conduct both ceremonies. The tsar and the tsarevich had already entered, followed and then encircled by the dignitaries of the military, the Holy Synod, the State, the Senate, and the highest-ranking members of the nobility.

After the first hour of prayers and sermons, Tatiana became more conscious of her surroundings. Tiers of icons formed the glittering iconostasis, creating a magnificent backdrop for floor-to-ceiling Corinthian columns swirled with lavish paintings and walls glowing with gold-trimmed frescoes. Tatiana, recalling her father's library, felt as if she stood inside of a gargantuan illuminated manuscript.

An archbishop blessed two filigreed wedding crowns held above Tatiana's and Alexander's heads throughout the ceremony, followed by himself and the tsar blessing the gold rings and the exchange of them. Despite the difficulty of doing so in their finery, the tsarevich and the new tsarevna prostrated themselves before the tsar, who then raised and gathered them in an embrace.

The coronation involved a series of rituals accompanied by Tatiana's donning of heavy royal regalia over her dress. Between the thousands of candles and lit candelabra, holy oils sprinkled on her head, incense shakers, and the oppressing weight of a symbolic scepter, orb, and crown, she felt a desire to flee for the forest at Tolkov.

After High Mass she curtsied again to the tsar, ensconced on a diamond-studded throne, then to her new husband, followed by the archbishop, patriarch, and metropolitan of the Orthodox Church.

Henceforth Tatiana would be known as Her Imperial Highness and princess or tsarevna of All the Russias.

As the couple exited the red velvet dais accompanied by a chorus of hymns, a grand pealing of bells, and seemingly endless salvos of cannon, the bride felt Alex's hand squeeze hers. If not for that comforting gesture, she might have imagined she had dreamed the entire day.

***

The combined nuptial and coronation rites had lasted five hours, and the festivities continued for another three days.

The first night's feast, however, was the most important and most elaborate. As a servant entered hoisting a platter with an entire roasted swan, Alex leaned toward her and whispered, "That is for you. It is a symbol of your beauty. And of fertility," he added, smiling at her.

She blushed. Not for the first time she wondered about Alex's first wife, Natalya. No one mentioned her, which seemed odd, and Tatiana could not help feeling curiosity about her predecessor. Had Alex indeed loved her as much as she had heard? How did the two women compare? Had he said similar things to her?

After she'd survived all the pomp, all the protocols, all the church services, all the celebrating and feasting, Tatiana knew she must face what she dreaded most: the wedding night.

In no time at all, they were escorted by a raucous group who told nasty jokes and stuffed the bride and groom with more food, according to tradition, before Alex and Tatiana were alone in their wedding chamber.

"Some wine, my lovely lady?"

She sipped gratefully, hoping it would relax her enough to tolerate exactly what she *thought* would happen next.

"I realize we scarcely know one another," he said softly. "If you prefer, we can talk a little."

Relieved, Tatiana told him about her father and her mother, and how each had taught her skills and knowledge about the forest. "I miss them both," she said quietly. "Even though my mother has been gone for nearly ten years now."

"I, too, grew up from the age of ten without my mother, who died in childbirth. I remember her well, though, and still always light a candle for her in church."

"I'm glad we can talk this way," she said almost shyly. Then she added boldly, "This cannot have been easy for you. Marrying someone you don't know, I mean."

"I admit that I was opposed to my father's insistence on the bride show. It has been done many times by previous tsars and princes, although I was terrified it would be a mistake. After Natalya died, I did not expect to care about another woman." His eyes looked sad for a moment, then twinkled. "Now I think my father might have been a genius."

"I hope so." Now she did blush. How could this man care about her after such a short time? And could she return his obvious feelings? And how could she hope to compete with Natalya?

"Did you know," he interrupted her thoughts, "that in older times the bride was not permitted to remove her veil on the wedding night? Nor to speak a word?"

"Truly . . ." Her voice trailed off in dismay. "Should we not—"

"That was then. This is now." Pulling her closer, he carefully removed the elaborate veil and then the headdress. "I would prefer to look upon your loveliness and especially your eyes. They remind me of the fire in an emerald."

Tatiana felt herself blush beneath the red paint that had been applied to her cheekbones and lips. Yet she could not stop herself from watching Alex slowly remove his silver brocade kaftan and all the wedding accouterments.

"It will be alright," he reassured her, and she knew exactly what he meant.

Alex obviously was experienced. Thankfully that meant he took his time, undressing her slowly and gently covering her entire body with kisses. Having never kissed a man on the lips, let alone have one touch her skin in intimate places,

Tatiana found it an amazing experience. His fingers gave her body sensations she had not felt before.

When at last he entered her, she winced at a few moments of pain, and Alex slowed before resuming the act. At first she remained nervous, before gradually beginning to enjoy the sense of this handsome naked man atop her.

After her groom groaned loudly and collapsed beside her, she decided she must have done something correctly. It was not at all the way she had imagined: it was much better.

In the morning Alex awakened her with more kisses, ready to start the process anew. This time, knowing what to expect, Tatiana relaxed. Now totally new sensations filled her body, and she met his moans with those of her own.

The newlyweds enjoyed a sumptuous breakfast in their chamber, with Alex smiling the entire time between bites and sips of tea. Tatiana could not help returning the smiles. Yes, she was happy, and satisfied. If this were marriage, it was way more gratifying than she had ever suspected.

The next few days passed in a blur: boat rides on the Moskva River, strolls in the gardens, long conversations in their chambers, visits to the kremlin churches to light candles and kiss icons, and so many servants ready to do her bidding that she barely noticed them anymore.

Only missing her father made her sad. Happily, Alex stayed beside her almost constantly.

Sitting on a bench in one rose-filled garden at the end of the week, her husband told her he had good news. "My Snow-drop has recovered fully, and I have asked her to join us out here. I do feel somewhat guilty for ignoring her more than

I should have. However, I have been awfully busy with my bride," he said, leaning to kiss her.

The properly veiled girl entered the garden awhile later, trailed by a bevy of similarly veiled ladies. "Your Imperial Highness," she greeted Tatiana smoothly after kissing her father's head. "It is my pleasure to meet you."

Tatiana had stood up and returned the girl's curtsy. "I look forward to becoming friends, Grand Duchess."

Snowdrop smiled and nodded, though it was a smile that did not reach her eyes. "Of course."

After that the conversation amongst the three evolved into one between father and daughter. Alex scolded Snowdrop for not taking enough care of herself. "You must do everything the royal physician demands." From that Tatiana suspected that Snowdrop had not done so, and somehow this suspected bit of rebellion endeared the girl to her.

"I have some knowledge of herbal remedies myself," she offered. "So if you ever need anything, Snowdrop, do not hesitate to call for me."

The girl's startlingly blue eyes seemed to bore into her own. "I doubt that will be necessary."

"This is wonderful news," Alex interjected. "I did not realize I had taken a healer for a bride."

"We shall see," Snowdrop said without expression.

"Snowdrop prefers to be referred to as Snow," Alex told his bride, grabbing his daughter's hand.

"No, call me Snowdrop," the girl said, firmly turning to Tatiana, who knew when she had been snubbed.

After Snow excused herself to return to her own apartments in the Terem Palace, Alex smiled at Tatiana apologetically. "She is not accustomed to strangers, having been sequestered so much of her life with nurses and servants. I hope to change such a system in the future, or at least permit the women to walk more often in the gardens or take more frequent carriage rides."

"I am grateful to hear this, Your Imperial Highness. As you know, I am accustomed to a lot of freedom and fear I will feel trapped as a caged bird in the terem day in and day out. And I already miss my personal maid, Olga, as well." *Not to mention my father*, she longed to add.

Alex threw back his head and laughed. "I see your point, my love. I shall have your maid sent to you if she is willing, and we will attempt to arrange excursions for you. No doubt my father and my advisors will complain, albeit comply eventually. I am beginning to feel so much affection for my darling bird," he said then, kissing her once more. "We must permit her some chances to fly."

"Thank you, Alex. And perhaps someday I will be permitted to hunt in the forest with you and your army."

"One thing at a time, my sweet. You don't want to give my men an apoplexy!"

It was enough for now.

***

His Imperial Highness frowned several times over dinner one night a few weeks later. They had elected to sup in his apartments and not the dining room, where Tatiana always felt uncomfortable sitting across from Snowdrop's critical gaze. The tsar occupied most of the fourth floor of the Terem Palace, yet there were so many alcoves and annexes that room had been made for the tsarevich's chambers, as well.

As for Snow, she remained on the entire third floor, normally assigned to the tsaritsa and her children. Since neither the tsar's wife nor Alex's wife had survived, Grand Duchess Snow remained where she had grown up. It had been assumed that Tatiana would share the third floor with her after spending the first month in her husband's chambers.

"Snow doesn't want to share," Alex then blurted out what so obviously was worrying him.

"Share what?"

"Her quarters in the Terem Palace. Normally that's where the royal women reside, and this is the time for you to begin spending your days there. It's quite palatial, and there should be more than enough room for the two of you and your ladies."

Somehow she was not surprised. "I don't mind," she told him, trying to ignore a niggling resentment.

"I must admit I never imagined myself being put in a position between my two ladies' desires."

"Isn't there a fine terem in one of the other palaces? Hundreds of us stayed in them during the bride show," she reminded him.

"Would you really mind that?" he asked hopefully.

"Not at all. And it would be all mine to decorate and furnish."

"True. I'm beginning to adore you, my sweet Tanya, and I just want you to be happy with me. When I travel I don't want to have to worry about quarrels between my new wife and my somewhat obstinate fourteen-year-old daughter."

Fourteen? Somehow all this time she had thought of

Snow as a diminutive eleven or twelve-year-old. Perhaps that explained her loathsome behavior and her disrespect—that and losing her mother at age thirteen *and* having a step-mother only four years older than herself thrust upon her.

"We'll pick a terem—or two or three of them—out for you then," Alex said with obvious relief.

Something else he'd said, however, concerned her. "When must you travel? And why?" she asked.

"With my father ill, it falls to me to tour the tsardom occasionally. And one never knows when enemies might lie in wait."

This was a topic discussed at Tolkov Castle rarely, as things had been peaceful throughout most of her father's lifetime. Yet she always hated the occasions when Sir Nicholas left for weeks or months. Now it sounded as if her new husband might do the same. "Do you anticipate a war?"

"Not soon, no. That does remind me that there is something important I must show you."

He stood and moved across the dining room to a huge tapestry embroidered with two silver unicorns. "Only a small number of people know this is here. In fact, only my guard, my father, my daughter—and now you."

Reaching up, he pushed on the left unicorn's horn. Stepping back, they watched as the tapestry swung outward to reveal what apparently was a hidden door leading to a staircase so steep you could not see the bottom.

"Astounding, is it not? It's a lengthy tunnel to safety in case of an emergency. If we are ever beset by enemies, this is where you must go immediately. Don't wait for me. Just be sure to pull the door shut."

"Where does it go?"

"All the way to the river. There are many iron doors you must go through to get there, however, and you will want to find a torch if possible to avoid all the false alcoves. Right now the doors are unlocked and will stay that way unless we are at war.

"In fact," he continued, "they say the entire Kremlin boasts a knot of secret tunnels, though most of them can no longer be located."

Tatiana was amazed and more than a little bit curious. Here, then, was an actual escape route that certainly might be useful whether during war or peace. She remembered her day in the Kremlin squares with Masha with fondness.

"I won't tell a soul," she promised.

Somewhat alarmed by the thought of enemies attempting to storm the palace via a hidden passage, she was also intrigued by the opportunity of using it to flee. She almost wished, however, that she didn't know about the secret exit.

Chapter 10

Months flew by, and Tatiana barely remembered her astounding trips to see Baba Yaga. Yet one day while sorting through the personal belongings stored since her wedding, she came across the sack filled with dried herbs, the vial of poison antidote, and the thick pewter mirror. She tried to remember what Baba had told her about it—something about safety or warnings perhaps.

She lived such a pampered and almost secluded life now she had nothing to fear other than that something might happen to Alex. However, she fretted about Snowdrop's continued stony stares, scowls, and snubs. There seemed no way to change their relationship to one of cordiality, let alone closeness. Fortunately, they only met a few evenings per week at dinner and during special church ceremonies. She suspected

Snow scheduled her prayers for a different time of day than when Tatiana and her ladies went, and that was fine with the new bride.

Not so new anymore, she thought, recalling that Alex had announced yesterday he and a small retainer would make their inspection of neighboring territories on the upcoming first day of spring. This, then, might be something to worry about. Perhaps to fear.

For the first time since Baba had given it to her, Tatiana examined the finely wrought mirror. Its long wide handle bore scrollwork of roses and lilies, and the mirror itself was encircled with chunks of cognac-colored amber. The back of the mirror, though, simply astounded her, embellished as it was with fine amber carvings in varying shades of honey, burnt umber, and fiery red. Each carving depicted a forest creature, including a frog, turtle, rabbit, owl, stag, and hedgehog that stood out in glorious orange, red, and sunflower hues against the pewter background.

Initially the mirror seemed to be nothing more than a decorative item. Suddenly, however, as she stared back at herself for a full minute, she heard a voice emanating from it:

Beware the one with golden hair
Who plots trouble for you to bear.

This had happened so unexpectedly that Tatiana nearly missed the words themselves. Now no matter how much she tried shaking the looking glass and squeezing its handle, it remained silent and would not repeat the couplet.

The girl with golden hair? She knew many, of course,

albeit only one prominent in her life: her stepdaughter Snow, with hair pale as spun gold. Plots? So far the girl had been an annoyance and a disappointment, nothing more—and certainly not a danger or someone the mirror should warn her about.

Nevertheless, she buried the looking glass below her finest chemises, knowing that the church regarded mirrors as demonic. As for the vial, in all these months she had dismissed worries of poison now that the bride show competitors and their families had long departed. The tsar himself had boyars who served as tasters to prevent poisoning, yet she and Alex had no such protection from any such evil-doers.

Starting today she would keep the antidote in her apron pocket or up one of her long sleeves at all times. Just in case.

***

Tatiana did not live in Terem Palace with the rest of the royal family and only dined there when summoned by Alex or the tsar. She loved her own apartments that now served as a terem for her and her ladies. The rooms were situated in a nearby palace overlooking two of the Kremlin's handsome brick towers, where Alex had ordered her spacious residence constructed from six smaller areas. Its narrow windows with thin sparkling mica panes gave her views of the river, as well. In part due to the efforts of stokers who visited hourly to keep three fires burning, and in part due to all the exotic Turkish tapestries hung on the brick walls, the rooms remained warm through the frigid winter. She especially loved her own place when Alex visited, although it meant Olga and her other ladies had to cover their faces as dictated by protocol.

After they departed or moved to an antechamber, the grand duke and duchess would sip glasses of rye-flavored *kvass* and nibble from platters of sugary confections topped with raspberries, currants, or strawberries. Here they might review one another's day, with Alex's always seeming infinitely more exciting.

"I wish I could accompany you and your men," she mentioned to Alex the day after she had discovered the power of the magic mirror.

"If wishes were diamonds, I could shower you with everything your heart desires, Tanya. Do you realize this must be the fifteenth time you have requested such an impossible thing?" He said it lightly, since they indeed had repeated this conversation countless times.

"I am useful in the countryside," she once again reminded him. "I can wield a bow and arrow, locate healing herbs, and fish the streams. And my riding skills are excellent so I could keep up."

"You know how inappropriate such a thing would be."

She did, of course, know that now. In the palaces noble and royal women remained mostly upstairs under lock and key in their terems, primarily because this is what the Church and its Patriarch mandated. Only country and city women of the lower classes had the freedom to walk about openly with their faces on public display. Her own upbringing had been an exception, as her parents and Tolkov's two clergymen paid scant attention to the lord's daughter's wanderings.

Occasionally she worked on a lengthy letter to her father, since the snows were melting and someone could get it to him in Tolkov. Olga had assured her that Sir Dimitri had remained in Moskva for the winter, so perhaps he would return to Tolkov and deliver it himself.

Not surprisingly, she found herself often bored, particularly as she was expected to occupy herself primarily with sewing. Unfortunately, being unskilled with a needle, she had no way to keep up with one of her primary roles: providing embroidered vestments, robes, tablecloths, etc. for the tsar's palace and Kremlin churches. She had solved the problem by assuming the position of overseer of both her own ladies and the royal seamstresses who toiled in other parts of the palace.

Her entertainments included being escorted to Terem Palace's golden throne room, where cloistered women could observe the tsar and the dignitaries he received from behind a curtained window in a balcony. There she could also listen to the beautiful music of flutes, balalaikas, accordions, and lutes—all forbidden inside the church where she was forced to go at least once a day, and certainly more than she wished.

Similarly, she enjoyed hiding behind a special screen overlooking the audience chamber and specially arranged for the imperial women. Below them boyars lined up in the same apparel she had noted at the bridal show: fashionable white damask robes, matching white knee-high boots, and white lynx or fox hats—all trimmed in gold. Ambassadors and dignitaries from other lands mingled with them, their appearances ranging from the nut-brown skin of the Cossacks to the more Asian features of the Tatars and their various delightfully colorful costumes.

Because the tsar had nearly retired from so many of his duties, she also had found one task she could assume on both the tsar's and the grand duke's behalf. This involved utilizing her writing skills to answer complaints and petitions brought before the tsar. His subjects sent these to their sovereign by means of a single narrow window in the tsar's study—known as the Petitioner's Window—which permitted them to stuff a small box with notes. Someone pulled it up and then lowered it daily.

Alex made most of the decisions if a reply were required or a dispute needed resolving, yet Tatiana found that she could do more than just write out his replies and have them dispatched. Some of the more negligible summons or suggestions she could respond to herself. After the limited experience she had had at Tolkov Castle under her father's supervision, she discovered that the Muscovites' problems were no more complex than those of her father's people.

However, it was also through this same box that someone had accused one of last summer's potential brides of using magic to make her extra beautiful. Tatiana had learned about this much later, and how it had resulted in the bridal contestant being dismissed—most likely for no cause. The box certainly had power.

Now Alex took advantage of the pride she took in her tasks. "How would my father handle all the petitions with neither of us here? And who would oversee all the new embroideries needed for the churches?"

"An excellent question, Your Imperial Highness. However,

I seem to recall such tasks still were completed for the year when you were a widow!"

As usual when she brought up his first wife or his life as a widow, Alex brushed the topic aside. "True, so maybe it's time you transferred some of these tasks to Snow."

Tatiana put down her quill and stared at him. "Snowdrop? Join me? Here?"

Alex looked uncomfortable. "Perhaps it is too soon. We can speak of this next year. Still, she is approaching fifteen now, and her ladies should take on some of the stitching, at least for the palace."

"It is a good idea. If you don't mind, my dearest, I'd rather they did so in Terem Palace, not here."

"I will speak to her for you if you prefer, my sweet. I tried to have her sufficiently educated—against the tsar's pro-tests—though I'm afraid her tutors did not think highly of her scholarly abilities. The Petitioner's Window, for example, is too important a task to delegate to a young girl. Nor can her handwriting compete with your fine skills."

She picked up her quill again. "Thank you, Alex. And I promise to stop asking about going to the forestlands with you and your army. Perhaps just the two of us sometime?"

"We shall see."

That seemed to be as much progress as she could make.

A week later Alex summoned her to his apartments, where they made love for the last time before his departure in the morning.

"May I bring you something back?" he asked afterward. "A gift for my beautiful princess?"

She thought a moment. "Some fresh mushrooms, straw-berries, and birch bark from the forest."

"That you shall have, my brave archer and forest nymph."

He propped himself on his elbow and stroked her hair. "I also want you to use my apartments as much as you want while I am gone. I know how much you enjoy time away from your terem and all the ladies, so I've instructed my guards to allow you total access."

"Thank you, Alex. That will help when I am working on the petitions." She knew by now that he trusted her to answer the simpler requests and to set aside any that required a decision after his return.

"And don't hesitate to approach my father or his council-ors anytime you desire or have need."

"As long as His Imperial Majesty is well. I hate to disturb him when he's having his bouts of illness."

"Of course." He kissed her deeply.

"Please be safe, Your Imperial Highness," she said, trailing her fingers over his shoulders and then chest.

"You, too," he said with a serious look. "I have ordered extra guards on the terems while I am away to ensure your safety."

"Thank you. I will be cautious," she promised, touched at his concern.

Before she left, he stopped her at the door for a final kiss. "May I ask a favor?"

"Anything, Alex."

"Watch over Snow? She needs guidance, and I'm afraid I continue to neglect her far too much."

"Of course." She said it with forced warmth, feeling as if a lump of ice had settled in her stomach. She no longer pitied the girl or longed for her friendship. Yet for the sake of the man she suspected she was growing to love after so many months, it seemed as if she could no longer avoid this implied duty. "I will visit her at the palace as often as possible."

It was the least she could do. And the best she could do.

Chapter 11

She had her ladies dress her with extra care for the visit to Snow, selecting a violet sarafan embroidered with golden lilies and fish. Amethysts covered her matching *kokoshnik* and strands of the same purple gemstone adorned her neck. For some reason she felt it necessary to remind the girl that she, Princess Tatiana, outranked the younger grand duchess. A princess the girl might be in name. However, it was her father and stepmother who would inherit the throne someday.

Not that I will rule over much, Tatiana realized. Women did not wear the crown except as a consort, unlike the situation in other countries that she had studied. Still, Alex valued her counsel and her education in a way she suspected was somewhat unprecedented in her country.

"Olga, please remind me to write to Sonya when I return. I owe her so much."

"Yes, Your Imperial Highness. She is a wonderful tutor—and a good friend. I miss her often."

Normally she insisted on less formality from her newly appointed chief maid of honor, yet there were others present. "Remind me, too, to ask my father if Sonya might be sent back to Moskva. Perhaps permanently, if she so desires."

"I know she would come with great pleasure, and there is no need at Tolkov Castle for a tutor anymore. Certainly there are no children."

The two smiled at one another, perhaps both with the same thought: hopefully someday soon there might be a need *here* for such a post.

This reminded Tatiana that no doubt Grand Duchess Snowdrop worried about that exact thing: a baby boy that would outrank her, as well. Alas, this was still not the case.

She could not deny her nervousness about interacting alone with Snow, however. No matter how much she tried to feel confident and courageous, she could not forget overhearing her vehemently ask the tsar not to select her to go forward in the bridal contest. She also recalled all the uncomfortable silences whenever the girl's name had come up from the servants and villagers back in Tolkov, so obviously the girl had a reputation.

Most especially, she could not completely disregard the warning from Baba Yaga's looking glass.

Nonetheless, she and her ladies—shielded by cloths held up before them—proceeded from their own quarters and across the square to the Terem Palace. She had sent Snowdrop a message yesterday announcing her impending arrival rather than merely sending a request that Alex's daughter could then ignore or deny.

Snow's ladies curtsied properly when they arrived, then withdrew to the other side of the room where Snow reclined in a throne-like chair. For a moment Tatiana feared that the grand duchess would ignore protocol. Thankfully then, she rose and proffered a half curtsy.

"I hope I find you well," Tatiana began.

Snowdrop—Tatiana had to remember that the girl specifically had asked her not to use her shortened name—stepped back a few paces and nodded.

"We are busy here," she said almost with a snarl. "In fact, there is too much stitching for myself and my ladies to accomplish. It is unfair." She waved around the room, where half-finished embroideries covered the chairs. As if to demonstrate, she returned to her own elaborate chair and picked up a threaded needle.

"I am sorry to hear it. Perhaps some of these tasks can be reassigned to the royal seamstresses."

"Good," she replied, jabbing her needle into a red linen cloth. "I find sewing revolting."

"I often feel the same." Tatiana forced a smile, relieved that here might be something the two had in common.

No response came and no invitation had been extended to her to sit. Tatiana did so anyway, settling herself at a table and then motioning all of her ladies except Olga to relax in an adjoining room.

Snowdrop's ladies, however, remained fixed as a row of statues standing stiffly along the richly painted walls. Only one moved forward to serve Tatiana and Olga glasses of tea in the traditional glass encircled by silverwork.

Remembering the mirror's warning, Tatiana only pretended to sip her tea. "Have you received a message from your father yet?"

Snowdrop shrugged. "No."

"Nor have I. I presume he is quite occupied and I would not expect him to spare one of his men to come so far back here simply to deliver a message."

She had meant to be reassuring. Apparently it was taken differently.

"We seldom correspond. Maybe you think you are different. I doubt you will hear anything before his own daughter does."

"Perhaps not." She reached into the middle of a silver fruit bowl. Snow apparently favored apples. Tatiana extracted a pear. Surely not all the fruit could have been poisoned. She suppressed a shudder.

"He wrote to my mother daily, you know," Snow said almost offhandedly. "They were so very close."

"Oh? What was your mother, the Grand Duchess Natalya, like?"

Snow smirked. "The most beautiful woman in the kingdom. She and my father were madly in love, you know. Well, of course you must know this. He could never love anyone else that way."

Tatiana felt her heart sink. Could this be true? She resolved to ask Alex, but did not wish to pursue this conversation with Snow, regardless of her curiosity. Or jealousy. Instead she merely shrugged as if to let her stepdaughter know that such statements did not concern her. "I'm thirsty," she said instead.

Snowdrop pointed at one of her ladies. "A glass of wine," she ordered and the girl scurried away nervously.

Now Tatiana noticed that not all of the wall statues were depictions of ladies; some were in fact human servants. Apparently, she maintained a much larger staff than her step-mother.

The rest of the visit remained stilted, with Snow barely replying to most of Tatiana's idle talk about palace affairs.

"I am wondering, Snowdrop, if a few of your ladies might want to come to the other palace—or perhaps to your father's apartments—and meet some of my own ladies. It might be interesting for all of them."

"My ladies have no time for such things. Thanks to you, we must stay occupied day and night." Before Tatiana could pro-test, Snow added frostily, "No one is permitted in the grand duke's chambers when he is absent."

"I am his wife."

"That gives you no such privileges."

"It does if your father orders it so," Tatiana said, inwardly seething at the disrespectful tone and words.

Snow shrugged. "Is there a specific reason for you to attend us today?"

"I just wanted to ensure you are well and happy. Your father asked me to do so out of love and concern, and I wanted to, as well."

"As you can see, I am absolutely fine. We do have many things to do, however, and my musicians will be here soon. It does make the work less tedious."

"I'm glad to hear that." Tatiana did not, however, rise to depart.

She admired the vaulted ceilings and tapestries before raising a subject that Alex specifically had asked her to bring up. "Quite soon your father and I will be discussing your bridal possibilities. Do you have any thoughts on this?"

"God's teeth! How dare you mention what is a matter between myself and my father only!" She rose and whirled out of the room, her uncovered golden hair flying behind in the breeze created by two little girls who had been fanning her.

Discouraged and not a little upset at the failure of her visit to mend any distrust between the two of them, Tatiana hastily clapped for her own ladies and quickly exited the rooms.

Olga, struggling to catch up with her mistress, sounded distressed. "Are you alright, my lady? Will you do anything to punish the grand duchess for such an insubordinate treatment of you?"

"No. Let us retire and order some of our own musicians."

That night she returned to Terem Palace to sleep in Alex's apartments, attended only by Olga and one other maidservant. She hoped someone saw her and would tell Snow.

Chapter 12

Weeks passed. Tatiana sent her stepdaughter a series of polite notes and greetings. The girl never responded. Occasionally when the tsar was feeling well they would all dine together, and only then did Snow manage some civility. Other than that, they communicated between themselves when necessary via Countess Tsergaya, who was in charge of protocol for both terems and most of the nobility.

Finally a letter from Alex arrived. Filled with news of the landowners' border disputes and churches he had visited, he also reassured her that he would return soon:

My darling, you have no idea how much I long for you. We have so much to discuss, and I miss you horribly. For now, though, there is some murmur-

ing from both the Poles and Swedes, and I need to ensure our borders remain secure and the tsardom does not return to a time of war and other troubles as we have in the past. In the meantime, I am send-ing one of my most trusted men (you will recall Sir Oleg) to attend to any needs you might have in palace affairs. He will also be the one providing my father with a full report. I fear so much for the tsar's health. Please send Snow my regards and love. I will write her soon.

Your beloved husband

The message cheered her, especially since Snowdrop had insisted that Alex had written daily to Natalya. Could she believe her? She resolved to get some answers from else-where. In the meantime, she dutifully conveyed Alex's mes-sage to Snowdrop via Countess Tsergaya. She also invited her stepdaughter to dine with her in Alex's apartments.

The grand duchess issued no response.

It was now full summer, with the nights lengthening and more opportunities to stroll the gardens with Olga and the rest of her ladies. She found herself longing for Alex most when she was out here, recalling all their conversations and stolen kisses behind the yews and morning glory vines. She had been here nearly a year, and other than missing her father, she felt content.

At times she and her retinue of ladies and maids would spend their morning in the enclosed gardens where they could enjoy swings and seesaws. She was permitted to invite female jesters, dwarfs, and clowns to entertain them, as well.

The most excitement for her and her ladies, however, presented itself via opportunities for carriage rides now that the muddy squares had hardened in the summer heat. Led by horsemen who scattered the people and livestock ahead, the procession of bright-red carriages with linen or sheer taffeta curtains nailed to the sides lumbered in a mostly circular route. Since noblewomen were forbidden to reveal themselves to men on the streets, though, the closed canopies and slit openings made it feel as if they were in moving prison cells. Yet it was a chance to view the city's bustling activity, and if she spotted something from behind the Kremlin's red and white walls, Tatiana could signal for the driver to halt and someone would purchase it for her from a shop or one of endless sleds loaded with merchandise. On fortunate days, she would get a carriage with sides made from thin animal bladders so she could see everything happening around her.

Sometimes she ordered just such a procession to convey herself and a few ladies on pilgrimages to nearby convents, including her favorite, The New Maiden's or Novodevichy. There she savored the companionship of the prioress and nuns, and inside the churches' cool stucco walls, embellished with gilded frescoes and icons, she felt at peace. The outside grounds, too, provided an opportunity to roam freely and to relish the cluster of gold, white, and blood-red buildings that gave the cloister the appearance of a series of elaborate layered cakes. She tried, however, not to think about all the royal women who had—and inevitably would—be forced by their husbands and male relatives to take the veil here.

As summer waned, the tsar seemed to feel much better and appeared so much heartier he could resume appearances.

Tatiana struggled to increase her activities to distract her from Alex's delayed return.

The work that seemed the most far behind was the now enormous pile from the petitioner's box. She had forwarded many of the more serious complaints to the tsar, filled an entire bowl with those awaiting the tsarevich, and kept the minor ones to tackle herself. Sir Oleg faithfully delivered the small box to her every other day now that the tsar again had need of his study.

It was on one such occasion when he had bowed, presented the box, and wheeled around smartly to exit Alex's quarters, that she called him back. "Your efficiency, kind sir, is admirable. You may, however, feel comfortable lingering long enough to speak or have tea."

Sir Oleg, a handsome man regardless of what appeared to be a saber scar down his jawline, blushed. "Of course, Your Imperial Highness. Whatever you wish."

"I wish," she said slowly, "to hear about my husband's travels and tasks, since he has been gone for months and I can barely envision his life when he is away from Moskva. Can you share some of your experiences together without betraying any confidences?"

He nodded uncomfortably, and she ordered a servant to bring them tea and sweets. She also stepped into the hallway to command one of the guards to come inside where he would take up his post to observe the proprieties.

"Have you served my husband for many years?" she asked, carefully choosing a sweetmeat from the platter.

"Since we were children, Your Imperial Highness."

"That is wonderful! Would you also share with me some stories about his childhood?"

He smiled and relaxed visibly, slowly and then more animatedly recounting some of the boys' adventures and exploits.

"We shall do this again if it pleases you," she said in dismissal. "And at times, I may ask you to deliver some of the more critical replies to petitioners."

"With pleasure. His Highness specifically requested that I be at your command in all things. And regardless of what you tell me or demand of me, Your Imperial Highness, I vow to keep silent about it. This is my promise to the grand duke. You have my fealty."

When he left, Tatiana felt as though she had made a new friend. Sonya was due to arrive soon, and Olga remained fiercely loyal. Sadly, her women friends had few freedoms in case she needed assistance that required leaving the palace. And as for Sir Dimitri, she assumed he had returned to Tolkov.

She resolved that the next time Sir Oleg delivered the box, she would attempt to get some answers about Natalya and Alex, and such an opportunity presented itself almost immediately. "Did her Royal Highness Natalya also handle the petitioner's box?" she asked as she motioned a servant to serve them tea.

"Oh, no, Your Highness. She kept to her own quarters nearly all the time. And to tell you the truth, it was better that way." Then, as if he realized he'd said too much, he complimented the fruit-filled pastries, his face turning almost as red as those same raspberries.

"Somehow," Tatiana said slowly, "I got the idea that the

two were inseparable. Madly in love, as they say throughout the kingdom."

Sir Oleg nearly choked on his pastry before hastily washing it down with tea.

"That was not true?"

He merely shook his head emphatically.

"They were a good match, I believe. Her family and his," she prodded.

When Tatiana attempted to pry a bit more, Sir Oleg hastily asked to be excused to "attend to urgent business."

The subject apparently was closed.

***

Another week passed, and Tatiana had caught up completely on the petitions. Often she sent off a letter or note with Alex's seal, demanding someone accused of stealing a neighbor's chicken or harness make recompense or suggesting that a woman who had lost her child or spouse pray to a certain saint. Other inquiries, such as a woman beseeching the tsar for a cure for barrenness or a man worried about his son's convulsions, she forwarded to one of the local healers or apothecaries. Simpler illnesses she handled herself, such as recommending beeswax and lemon peel for scurvy or feverfew leaves and chickpea paste for muscle aches.

In so many ways the other pleas for help and squabbles reminded her of the work she had done sitting beside the father she still missed dreadfully. He wrote that he missed her terribly, too. "I dared not leave Tolkov during the planting or harvesting seasons." She knew he also wanted to avoid the tsar, whose offer to make him part of the royal retinue had been declined politely. A new position would have served as a traditional bridal gift for her family, yet she knew her father would never leave Tolkov unless the tsar commanded it. Fortunately, His Majesty's frequent illnesses kept him preoccupied.

Her mind on her father, Lord Alexander, she did not at first register the content on the petition in front of her. For one thing, it was not unusual for a petitioner to accuse someone of sorcery, and most of these she responded to by promising an investigation (which usually solved the problem), suggesting that the supplicant employ a countermeasure, or saving it for Alex if it were more serious.

This one shocked her:

His Royal Majesty, I regret to inform you that Grand Duchess Snowdrop Alexanderevna has sinned against God and the tsardom's people. She is a sorceress who lusts after a huntsman. Please stop her for the sake of her soul and ours.

It was unsigned, as accusations often were, and thus normally would be taken less seriously. Yet this was no ordinary allegation about suspected magic that involved someone interfering with a neighbor's blacksmith business or thieving of a loaf of bread or inexplicably causing illness to someone's pig. And this was of course no ordinary accused: it was the royal princess!

Shocked, Tatiana read and reread the brief note. Snow? Sorcery? Lusting? How would she have an opportunity to engage in the latter while virtually locked in Terem Palace? True, there was an underground passageway from Terem Palace that Snow's ladies used to reach the church during winter months, but it was usually crowded since services ran continually from dawn to dusk.

It took only a few minutes for her to dismiss her servants and approach the unicorn tapestry. It opened smoothly, having obviously not been used recently since a thick circle of cobwebs blocked the second stair. She reclosed the heavy door carefully.

If not here, where and how?

And then she recalled Alex's speculation that many such secret exits might exist in the Kremlin's buildings.

Could there be one in Snow's quarters? How would she, Tanya, find out? Surely no man could make frequent visits to Snow without gossip filtering through the imperial household.

Unfortunately, there was no way to trace the unsigned petition to its owner, and most of those who submitted them hired someone to write for them—leaving no handwriting clues to pursue.

Dispatching a messenger to summon Olga at once, she knew if there was a modicum of truth to the charge she must act fast—and certainly before Alex returned.

***

She showed the note to Olga, who blanched. "Can this be true? She's a rude and conniving girl, but witchcraft?"

Now might have been the time to confide in Olga about her encounters with Baba Yaga, yet she would not. Allegations of sorcery or witchcraft often led to the accused's exile or even death if the church discovered them. Still, most of the Russian people believed in magic. It was an interesting blend, Tatiana often had mused, which might be why such denunciations were rare. Everyone simply accepted that regardless of what the clergymen said, sorcery could and did exist in some form.

"Do you know what has happened to Sir Dimitri?" she asked.

"No, My Lady, yet I suspect he might be back here in Moskva—if he ever left. He seemed determined to stay here for your father's sake to watch over you."

"Yet I have never seen or even heard from him."

"I believe that is the way he desires it so that he can better ensure he monitors any threats or dangers to you." Tatiana imagined that she saw Olga blush.

"What kind of dangers?" She was touched—and puzzled.

"I do not know, my dear Tanya. He is a knight and undoubtedly has access to much information."

"Then perhaps he can help."

"In what way?"

"Olga, can you manage to borrow a servant's clothing and get out of the castle unnoticed?"

"I can, Your Imperial Highness."

"Excellent. Then you must discover whether Dimitri or any of my father's knights are here. Bind them to silence and see what they can find out about any huntsman who might have access to Snow's quarters or her person. I'm not certain how they can accomplish this, only that we must try."

Olga returned that evening, once again dressed in a proper outfit marking her as one of the grand duchess's entourage. "Sir Dimitri begs me to assure you that he is at your service. He is investigating based on what I told him and will get word to one of us when he can. Sirs Mikhail and Igor shall return soon, as well."

Somewhat reassured, Tatiana would wait. She had considered confiding in Sir Oleg, although she had no idea if his loyalties would lie with her if her needs were pitted against those of his prince's daughter. She must discover the truth herself.

Chapter 13

Three days later, Olga slipped into Tatiana's room first thing in the morning. "Before you break your fast, My Lady, we must talk. I have asked all the servants and the other ladies to depart."

Tatiana sat up, the blue velvet bed curtains now open, and motioned for Olga to perch on the edge of the bed.

"Here's what Sir Dimitri knows," Olga began. "There are two logical suspects. Both are unmarried; only one recently has flaunted a lot of coins—many more than he earns in service to the court. The other huntsman merely has acted unusually secretive and almost joyful for no apparent reason. Both also have disappeared for long periods of time without leave."

"Hmmm. My best estimate would be the one with the extra

coins to spend. I cannot imagine a man feeling 'joyful' over a relationship with the tsarevna unless she has promised to promote him somehow."

"These are Sir Dimitri's thoughts exactly. He will keep a close eye on both, however, and report to you when he knows something. He suggested an 'accidental' meeting in the main rose garden a week from today."

Relieved, Tatiana resumed her daily routine, which even included dinner with Snowdrop and the tsar the following evening.

Alex's father obviously had improved dramatically, and wore his sable-trimmed crown studded with pea-size diamonds while he ate. The meal seemed to last forever, as members of his council of boyars had joined them. Lords in waiting stood silently and attentively behind each chair.

Women were expected to eat silently. Near the end of the twenty-course meal, however, the tsar looked across the table and actually smiled at her. "My dear Princess, I have had excellent reports about your assumption of some of the prince's duties—in particular the minor petitions. My son will be most pleased upon his return."

"Thank you, Your Imperial Majesty. You are too kind." She was careful to keep her eyes lowered, as it was forbidden to look the tsar in the eye without special permission. He already had turned his attention elsewhere, particularly when three servants arrived balancing a giant sugar confection carved in the shape of the entire Kremlin.

On the appointed day, Tatiana made sure to include only Olga and one other lady on her stroll through the heavily trellised rose garden. There she frequently rested on one of the marble benches, so no one suspected anything when a fine-looking, brightly appareled knight happened to be passing by and knelt before her as if in obeisance.

"Your Imperial Highness," Sir Dimitri said loudly, then lowered his tone. "It is so good to see you once more. I pray you are happy?"

"I am. And you, kind sir? I understand you have been cognizant of my welfare, and I must thank you."

"No need, Tat—I mean, Your Imperial Highness. I must mention that everyone comments on how you add much beauty and grace to the imperial court. I also must tell you, however, that your father misses you terribly, as does everyone at Tolkov." His voice trailed away as he remained on one knee.

"I miss all of you, too," she replied, loosening her veil just enough to see his face more clearly. She would have loved to exchange pleasantries and perhaps have a long conversation with her relative. Then she noticed her other lady watching before Olga attempted to lead her to the far side of the garden.

She motioned for Dimitri to sit beside her so no one could overhear them, and prayed the Countess Tsergaya did not stroll by, leading a group of trainees who trailed her everywhere like ducklings behind their mother.

"And the mysterious huntsman?" she asked softly.

"I believe there may be truth to the rumors. One of them spends money freely, and also seems to have grown remarkably religious in the past months. I am told by a priest that he worships often now—remarkably more often than previously—although he seems to disappear and reappear at odd intervals."

"And what do you suspect?"

"That if there is any truth to the rumor or the accusation, then perhaps he—his name is Ivan Ivanovich—is meeting the young princess via a special entrance or exit in the church. The priest seemed unaware of any such mysterious methods of entry, however, and I did not tell him anything more than that one of our huntsmen seemed to be acting suspiciously. The father promised to be discreet while keeping an eye out for Ivan."

"That is as much as we can hope for, Dimitri. I will intensify my efforts to find the passage entry from inside the palaces."

He bowed and kissed her hand. "Farewell for now, My Lady."

***

It took days for Tatiana to work out her plan, and she knew she must conduct her investigation before Alex returned. Fortunately, her hints to Countess Tsergaya bore fruit: Tatiana had suggested that Grand Duchess Snowdrop take her ladies to Novodevichy Convent before the weather turned cooler.

"She should bring all of them with her," she added to the countess. "I worry that her ladies get little air, and I also fear for their souls. I will advise the prioress and the nuns to look for them on Thursday."

Countess Tsergaya seemed pleased at this attempt to encourage more piety, and Tatiana spent Wednesday evening with only Olga, the two of them dining and sleeping in her husband's apartments one floor below Princess Snowdrop's terem.

As soon as Olga reported the following morning that all of Snowdrop's retinue appeared to have departed, she and Tatiana approached the entrance to the terem.

"I must inspect this last batch of embroideries," she said blithely to the sole guard left on duty in the women's absence. "And I wish not to be disturbed," she added in her most regal tone.

He bowed and closed the door behind them.

Now it was a matter of searching. Without telling Olga about the secret passageway in Alex's bedchamber, she explained that they needed to find a hidden way out of the terem. Olga began to search the furniture and floorboards, and Tatiana the walls in every room.

Convinced such an exit existed, she prayed only that they would discover it before Snow's return. Thankfully no one interrupted them.

Only an hour later she found it.

"Look!" she exclaimed to Olga.

It was in Snow's bedchamber. At first she had almost skipped over a somewhat ugly tapestry portraying three giant bears amidst some spruces. It was only after pushing on several areas that she discovered that the right eye of the middle bear caused the wall behind it to move slightly.

And there it was.

"I must follow this secret passageway, Olga," she said excitedly. "It is the only way I can determine where it leads. I suspect it might be inside one of the cathedrals. Can you stand watch for me?"

"My Lady, what if they return?"

"It is too early. And I know I risk much, although if it comes out where I think it does, I should be able to slip back into my own rooms without detection."

Olga shivered. "Go then, yet wouldn't it be much safer if I went in your place? No one would notice me."

Tatiana was determined. She had to see this tunnel—which it appeared to be—for herself.

"Be sure you depart just before the guard does and advise him I am taking a small rest," she reminded Olga. "The guards change in an hour, so hopefully no one will be certain whether or not I left. The ladies in our palace believe I am at Alex's apartments, so no one will seek me. And make sure this secret door is shut behind me and the tapestry put back in place. If I have trouble, I will return and tap on the inside of the hidden door."

And so she went, at first slowly and carefully lest she fall. She had had Olga pile her hair up atop her head and brought along a hat to cover it. Just in case, beneath her sarafan she wore a tunic and breeches in the style of western visitors. Now she paused to don her disguise and hang her other clothing over her arm as if she carried a cloak.

The passageway was indeed a tunnel, and a flat one at that. She speeded up on the brick floor.

There were no doors, such as Alex had described, along the route to the river. The tunnel actually wound around and around so that no one could see you up ahead or observe you coming at them even though lit sconces partially illuminated portions.

It took her only roughly ten minutes, her heart pounding so hard she felt as if a bell ringer were shaking her insides.

When the tunnel yielded natural light, Tatiana knew she had arrived.

She almost ran right into it: a rose trellis.

Just beneath her feet she could make out a long dress—a sarafan—strewn against the wall. It must be Snow's disguise. Afraid to disturb the cloth, she peered through the leaves.

Realizing at once no one strolled the garden at this moment, she slid between the still blooming rose bush and hurried toward the palace entrance to avoid detection.

Only when she safely had reached her own palace did she realize how much risk she had been taking recently. The trellis blocked a garden entrance that overlooked the exact bench on which she and Sir Dimitri had sat only days ago!

Chapter 14

Tatiana waited patiently. Then impatiently. She had decided to stay silent and out of sight until she was certain no one had learned of her secret visit to Snow's terem. She also needed to ensure that her own absence had gone unnoticed.

Fortunately, all remained calm. Sir Oleg delivered a message that Alexander would return within days, which added a sense of urgency to the rest of her mission.

"Please summon Sir Dimitri to the morning glory garden," she told Olga, mindful of the fact that the main rose garden was visible from the secret tunnel.

He came the next day after Tatiana had advised Countess Tsergaya that she needed to hear a report from him about her father and affairs in Tolkov, to which she was still the heir.

Dimitri remained on one bended knee for their short conversation, a position Tatiana feared had to be uncomfortable.

"I discovered the tunnel," she said quickly. "It does not lead to the church. There must be a secret means of getting from there to the rose gardens, however."

"I'm not certain that matters if they use different routes. The fact is that somehow they are using the garden for their meetings, and presumably he then takes her elsewhere."

"I cannot let her father learn of this."

"Do you want me to rid His Imperial Highness of the problem?" he offered.

"You don't mean—"

"No, no. Even her father would not have him killed, although he would certainly end up in the dungeon."

"Then the huntsman must go," she said firmly. "I want him out of her life so there is no more temptation and no more opportunities for her to get caught." *Though it would serve her right,* she thought for the dozenth time.

"I can exile him, except that requires permission from someone—and would involve an explanation."

"No, it would be too much of a scandal." She thought for a moment. "You must warn him certain members of the palace staff have learned that he might be involved with the young tsarevna, and that his life is therefore in danger."

Her youngest cousin's prematurely weathering face looked grim. "This I can do. I will command that he leave Moskva immediately or face possible death when the grand duke returns."

"Do it. Ensure he leaves at that moment. Give him no chance to meet with her—or send a message—and thus reveal our involvement. If she learns who approached him, she will suspect me immediately. For the sake of her father . . ."

"I understand, Your Imperial Highness. The huntsman will be gone tonight."

Nervous about what she had set in motion, she was nonetheless thrilled when, before leaving, Dimitri presented her a letter from her father.

"I miss home sometimes," she told him, clutching the letter to her heart.

"As I have said before, I can assure you that you are much missed, as well." He stood, bowed low, and left the garden quickly.

***

Alexander's return was a joyous occasion for the entire court, and the first evening the tsar ordered a thirty-course dinner in his son's honor. Snowdrop sat on the opposite side of Alex, munching on apples—her favorite fruit—so Tatiana did not have to face her.

She is so gorgeous, with that perfect pale, yet naturally glowing skin, Tatiana thought when the grand duchess arrived. In fact, she had never looked lovelier. The girl resembled a well-fed Madonna haloed in brightness and beauty. She wished things could be different between the two of them.

For several days Tatiana stayed with Alex in his apartments, and they resumed their lovemaking, as well as long talks about his adventures over the summer. He spoke freely with her about potential war, troubles along the border, his knights' bravery and exploits, and his continued concern about his father's health.

Sometimes, however, Tatiana thought their relationship was too cautious. For one thing, she remained curious about her predecessor, Grand Duchess Natalya Sergeievna. Perhaps Alex never brought her up to avoid hurting Tatiana. Yet there were things a somewhat jealous second wife might want to know.

Still, she and Alex had never been happier. The "problem" with Snow had been solved, and she was relatively certain Alex would never learn of his daughter's indiscretions—and the huntsman's treason to the crown.

One afternoon Alex invited Snow to join them for tea, and Tatiana resolved to find a way to demonstrate that the two of them were reconciled—from what, she did not know. Certainly the fact that she had brought up the subject of the girl's marriage prospects had exacerbated their mutual enmity.

This time it was Alex's turn to raise that same subject.

"I'm not ready to wed!" Snow insisted, setting her glass down so hard it nearly splintered.

"For the sake of the tsardom," Alex stressed the last word, "you must do so in the next two years."

Tatiana felt some real sympathy for the girl. After all, she herself had resisted the idea of marriage when she was only a few years older than Snow. The fact that she had ended up a married woman was due to an odd and unexpected circumstance.

"Perhaps she is too young for this conversation," Tatiana tried to intercede and calm the girl.

"You! Stay out of this. You are not my mother! And I am certainly not too young—only unwilling!" Her beautiful features twisted in anger at her stepmother, and this time even Alex saw a glimpse of that hatred.

"Snow!" Alex scolded her. "Tsarevna Tatiana may not be your mother. However, she has your best interests at heart. And you must realize that the two of us will consult on potential grooms."

"But she—"

"She is my wife, and I will not have you showing such disrespect!"

"May I be excused, father?"

"Not without an apology to Tatiana."

For a few moments Tatiana believed that such a thing was impossible, and she knew if just the two of them were in the room, no apology would ever be forthcoming.

Snow stood and curtsied. "I beg pardon of Your Imperial Highness."

After she left, Alex paced the room. "Was I too harsh, Tanya?"

"*Nyet*, I do not believe so. And you are correct that we must have heirs to the throne."

"Tanya—is it possible that you and I could soon provide one?" He sounded hopeful on the subject they usually avoided. Certainly he had attended to his bedding duties with boundless enthusiasm.

"I pray it will be soon, My Lord."

"As do I," he said, and stopped pacing to kiss her. "Would my love indulge me in a game of chess?"

"She would." Tatiana smiled. Deep inside she said a small

prayer that perhaps her monthlies would stop soon and she could give Alex the news he so longed to receive.

***

In early autumn, Tatiana began suffering bouts of morning sickness. The kingdom's and Alex's wish had been fulfilled and her own prayers answered sooner than she had expected. Yet she was not entirely certain she was ready to be a mother. As an obviously unsuccessful stepmother, she feared she might fail at motherhood, as well.

Alex was elated and solicitous from the moment she told him of the pregnancy. She had hoped to keep the blessed news a secret at least for a short time. Instead it spread potentially from her laundress through the court and from there to the countryside faster than the usual salacious court gossip.

Now there was to be another celebration banquet—a dual festivity, since it was Snow's fifteenth birthday. Tatiana had turned nineteen that summer. For some reason everyone had forgotten.

If Snow resented sharing her special day with Tatiana, however, she did not reveal it. In fact, she seemed unusually cheerful, even proposing a toast to the upcoming birth.

"I look forward to meeting my new younger sister or brother in early summer," she announced, following this with a cheerful *"Na Zdorovie!"* Snow managed a convincing smile that puzzled Tatiana. Either this baby would be the one thing that might mend the enmity between the two of them, or Snow was a skilled liar.

The festive dinner lasted for hours, and due to the twin celebrations, the tsar had elected to have it held in the elaborate banquet hall in the Palace of the Facets. Tatiana lost track of all the courses served, barely noticing the richly dressed servants circling around a massive gold pillar that dominated the hall. Fortunately, her stomach did not upset her as the servants brought gold plate after gold plate of such things as roast stork with sweetmeats, grouse with plum sauce, cocks dressed with ginger, saffron-basted hares, marshmallow-covered larks, sturgeons, and peacocks with tails fanned out behind them on the trays.

Between each course she imbibed the traditional palate-cleansing beverages of cherry spirits, black currant liqueurs, juniper, and mead, along with French and Hungarian wines, flavored vodkas, and kvass.

Everything seemed cordial, and Tatiana began to relax as she watched the jesters and listened to a musician strumming a *gusli*. Between desserts, Tatiana again tried to imagine what had inspired Snow's new attitude.

Still wondering late that evening, Tatiana returned to her terem and ladies. Sonya had joined them two nights earlier, and now that she was settled into her new quarters, Tatiana was anxious to hear the latest news from Tolkov.

An hour later, while she, Sonya, and Olga were discussing Cook Maria's new romance with the village bookseller, Tatiana unexpectedly leaned over the table and retched roast duckling with cherry sauce all down her night shirt.

"My Lady!" Olga leaped up and held her head up and her braids back.

Sonya hurried across the room to retrieve some cloths and dip them in the water basin.

"You ate too heavily, Your Imperial Highness," she ventured as she began to clean up, motioning for two other servants to bring a clean gown. "Should I summon a physician?"

"*Nyet*," Olga insisted. "I will make her a special tea."

Now sweating profusely, Tatiana began to panic. *Could she be losing her baby so soon?*

"I will be fine," she assured everyone, before suddenly she began vomiting again.

Now terrified, her mind flashed back over the day's and night's activities. She had eaten and drunk so many items that if one were tainted, how would she identify which? And she had never had food tasters as the tsar did.

"Olga! I need some help," she said as calmly as she could manage.

"Yes, My Lady. Anything."

"What can we do?" Sonya demanded.

"Go into my bedchamber and retrieve the gown I wore tonight. No one should have taken it away yet, and inside one of the sleeves is a small bottle that I must have. Hurry!"

Olga returned in less than a minute, and Tatiana gratefully sprinkled a few drops on her tongue. She waited only moments for them to dissolve.

"What is that?" Sonya asked.

"It's for poison, isn't it?" Olga whispered so that the other ladies now huddling around her did not hear.

"Please tell no one."

Sonya and Olga wisely dismissed all the ladies. Someone already had summoned a physician, who arrived all too soon with his blood-letting equipment and two large cloths to hide the grand duchess's skin from his view. Most men were forbidden to touch a royal woman, and even doctors used females to assist them.

Finding herself feeling better, Tatiana ordered him away before he began to bleed her.

"Your Imperial Highness—"

"I said you must depart. I ate something cooked improperly. There is no way to identify the tainted food. I have my own herbs, as you may recall, and am much recovered now."

Mumbling to himself and then making one more attempt to persuade his grand duchess to be examined, he left the terem.

The three women retreated into the imperial bedchamber and closed the door.

"It was Snowdrop," Olga said quietly. "I know it."

Sonya was shocked. "Snowdrop? Why on earth would the princess do such a horrible thing? I know she has a reputation for cruelty, yet surely not this!"

Olga tried to explain things briefly, at least about the petitioner's warning and the secret tunnel, while Tatiana took deep breaths and tried to stop her trembling.

"We must report this to someone," Sonya insisted. "To the grand duke, if no one else."

"I don't think he would believe me," Tatiana ventured weakly. "Why would anyone believe this?"

"Are you certain?" both women asked in unison.

"Yes. The potion I took is specifically made to counteract poison. Without it I could have died—or at least lost the babe."

"How did you know the liquid would work?" Sonya asked.

She hesitated. "It was given me by an apothecary I met

who promised it would be useful if I became involved in dangerous circumstances."

The other two looked soberly at one another, then back at her. Tatiana knew they believed her now. She had no such confidence that they would if she had told them she had received the potion as a gift from a real witch.

"You must sleep," her two trusted ladies from Tolkov urged her.

It took her hours to do so, however, as questions whirled through her head. Of course it would not have been difficult to bribe one of the serving staff at the banquet. That part made sense. Yet why wait until now? Tatiana had been Snow's stepmother for a year. Could it be only because of the pregnancy? Did she see it as a threat to her own grasp of power if she herself were to marry a nobleman who might take the throne on her father's death? A husband who might impregnate her with a rival son?

Now the meaning of Snow's smile tonight meant something different than reconciliation. And to think the princess had had the audacity to toast to Tatiana's and the baby's health!

She did fall asleep, yet only after drawing one conclusion: she could never tell her husband that his own daughter may have attempted to murder his wife.

Chapter 15

From her terem windows, Tatiana gazed at the last of the gold, topaz, and ruby-colored leaves drifting slowly through the air, then whirling faster as autumn winds increased and leaves carpeted the Kremlin's squares. White pigeons lazily circled the cupolas or hopped around the ground. It was in the fall that she most missed the forest.

All too soon heavy snow capped the red brick towers and frosted the cathedrals' golden and silver cupolas. How she longed to take sleigh rides along the ivory and burgundy Kremlin walls or stroll through the imperial gardens. She imagined branches iced like diamond swords and bushes transformed into glittering jeweled crowns the way they had appeared during winters in Tolkov.

Going out was impossible now. If she had felt constrained

before, that had been nothing compared to the restrictions placed upon the pregnant mother of a future royal heir. Even church services—once required twice a day standing behind a screen overlooking the cathedral's candles, icons, and frescoes—were denied. Alternatively, she was encouraged by Countess Tsergaya to pray regularly at the traditional Red Corner near the entrance to the terem. There she could light candles, bow in prayer, repeatedly cross herself, and kiss the arrangement of saints' icons.

Christmas and the Epiphany came and went. Days dragged slower than most winter seasons. Only her rapidly swelling belly assured her time actually was passing.

In the terem, the presence and company of Olga and Sonya were her salvation. Ignoring Countess Tsergaya's displeasure, Sonya regularly secured books and drawing materials. Since Tatiana's sewing skills remained far inferior to those of her entire entourage of ladies, she often read aloud to them as they dutifully stitched gowns and embroidered church vestments.

She did, however, enjoy the two blind storytellers who recounted or sang epics and tales of heroes, knights, and the various characters she'd read about before leaving Tolkov. Her favorites were those about the multi-plumed mythical firebird, the Tsarevna Vasilissa, and of course, Baba Yaga. Since she knew the latter truly existed, why not some of the other characters in these stories?

Tatiana did miss her husband, who rarely summoned her to his apartments after the first couple of months for fear of risking the life of the child. She sent pleading notes: "I beg you, Your Imperial Highness, to reconsider your denial of my presence. I am suffering enormously from lack of your companionship and your kisses." "I assure you that I could have a litter safely transport me to the Terem Palace." "Could I not dismiss my ladies, and you could see me here in the terem rather than deny me your company?"

He refused her requests. He did, however, write loving messages that should have appeased her. Still, it wasn't fair. She knew pregnant women were not expected to present themselves in public, which she could barely accept. She also recalled that she would be forced to spend forty days after the birth without leaving her bedchamber to be considered cleansed in the Church's eyes.

***

In the end, none of it mattered.

She lost the baby just before Maslenitsa, the festival officially marking the end of winter and the advent of Lent. As she suffered the attentions of three imperial midwives and later two royal physicians sent by the tsar to fuss over her, she tried to imagine the activities in the countryside. At home, as she still thought of Tolkov, Cook Maria would be baking hundreds of pancakes. For an entire week everyone would partake of sleigh rides, festivities, music, dancing, gift exchanges, sledding, skating, and even snowball fights. Idly she wondered what celebratory events might be happening right now in the Kremlin's squares.

Such thoughts did not offer the escape she longed for.

Her husband, the tsar, the court, and all of Moskva and those outside the city who had heard the news mourned with her. Condolences poured in from the court, the people, and diplomats from multiple kingdoms.

Tatiana didn't know if it had been a boy or a girl, and the midwives had cleaned her up and removed the blood and the afterbirth without telling her anything whatsoever.

"I feared losing you more than the loss of the child," Alex assured her. "We will still have our baby, just not as soon as we had expected."

She felt relieved that her husband didn't scold her for moving around too much or failing to pray often enough. She had heard Olga on more than one occasion chastising one of her ladies or servants for such murmurings.

Olga and Sonya remained convinced that the poison early in the pregnancy had caused her to miscarry.

"Or it could have been the antidote," Sonya dared to suggest.

"You must tell the grand duke now—or perhaps the tsar—about the poison," Olga urged.

"I cannot. It would cause irreparable harm to the family's relationship, blame on me, and a sentence of treason for her."

"It was her deviousness and intent to murder you that could have caused the poor babe to die!"

Tatiana did not believe Sonya's assertion, although it might have been easier to assume Snow's culpability. Deep down she suspected the miscarriage had occurred too long after the incident, and she did not accept that Baba would have given her something that dangerous to counteract the poison. Plus, they still had no proof Snow was behind the attempted poisoning—merely a strong suspicion.

In fact, she knew where to place the responsibility.

"It is my fault, husband," she said tearfully. They were playing chess and it was only the second time since the miscarriage that the doctors had granted permission for her to walk across the square to Alex's apartments.

"It was in God's hands," he assured her, pausing in his next chess move to look across the table. When he noted the tears streaming down her cheeks, he rose and gathered her to him on the sofa. "God chose to take our child for his own. There is no blame."

"He was punishing me!" she cried.

"Whatever for?"

"For resenting—not the child, just all the restrictions the pregnancy placed on me."

Alex shook his head and attempted to dry her tears with his sleeve. "That is nonsense."

"It is the truth. Every day I wished for the baby to arrive soon—and the forty days of seclusion after the birth to pass— so I could move around freely. Don't you see?"

"*Nyet*, I don't. I can only imagine that every woman who is with child feels the same at times."

"Can you ever forgive me?"

"I told you before, my dearest. The fact that you are here in my arms and not buried beside my Natalya is the greatest gift Our Lord could bestow."

"Truly?"

"Truly. And as soon as your body has healed completely, we will create another child. And then another, God willing."

"I pray it is so, Alex."

"It will be. And in the meantime . . ." Grinning somewhat

mischievously, he reached into a mahogany bureau and from it produced a velvet bag. "For you, my precious."

"A gift? Why now?" She swallowed hard, willing it not to be a consolation prize for losing the baby.

"Because your husband has been a foolish man—so foolish and neglectful that he failed to ask just once when your birthday might be." For a moment he looked crestfallen. "I will always blame myself for celebrating my daughter's birthday and sadly not my wife's."

"It passed last summer, so—"

"That is no excuse. And just in case I am away on your twentieth birthday *this* summer, I selected two gifts for you."

Tatiana reached into the bag curiously, extracting two items carefully wrapped in silk. "My God!" she pronounced, as first a giant emerald dangling from a gold pendant and then a pair of matching emerald earrings rimmed by diamonds fell into her hands.

"To match the green fire in your eyes, of course," Alex murmured, watching her carefully as if uncertain she would like them. "Will you forgive me for my neglect?"

"I love these! How could I feel you are neglectful when you went through this trouble?"

"Because I never want to do anything except treasure you, and if I ever fail to do so again, you must chastise me fitfully. Promise?"

"I promise," she vowed. She nearly added the three words she knew he must long to hear—*I love you*—but at the last moment kept them to herself. She knew he loved her, and for now that was the most important thing.

Reassured of that and that she was faultless in the loss of

her child, she determined to resume her life as Her Imperial Highness Tsarevna Tatiana Nicolaievna with as much enthusiasm as she could find within herself.

***

No word of condolence, let alone greeting, came from Snowdrop. In fact, it was rumored that she had locked herself in her bedchamber attended by only two ladies.

This did not bother Tatiana, yet apparently offended Alex. "My daughter has no right to seclude herself even further from court," he complained. "I didn't expect her to be so heartbroken about what happened, yet can think of no other explanation."

Except that her earlier devious plans had been thwarted, Tatiana thought. Still, Snow could not know that she was a suspect, so why lock herself up? Unless, of course, she scarcely could contain her joy over the loss of the baby.

Eventually Tatiana and Alexander resumed their dinners with a visibly defeated yet sympathetic tsar. "You will have many other children, my son and daughter," he weakly tried to reassure them. Yet both knew how much the possibility of another male heir had disappointed him given his intermittent bouts of sickness.

"We have plenty of time, father," Alex tried to reassure him. "And Lord willing, you will be with us for so long that we will have the leisure to create many more children."

The tsar pushed back his raspberry dessert. "*Da*, perhaps you are correct. It is also time to marry the princess to a nobleman who could increase our chances. Do you not agree?" He stared intently across the table. Both of them looked down.

"The tsarevna claims not to be prepared yet for marriage," Alex dared offer.

"God's knees! She is fifteen years old and knows exactly what her duty is!" the tsar railed. "Send her to me and I will point out the facts if you two cannot arrange someone suitable for her—and soon!" His face reddened, and Tatiana feared for his health again.

"I will do so, Your Imperial Majesty," Alex promised. "As soon as she makes an appearance in court. At the moment, however, she seems to be ill—or in mourning for the lost child."

"Then she has three more days to present herself. It seems to me your daughter is sick much too often, and I have my suspicions that she mopes in her terem for no good reason. She must marry into our kingdom rather than to one of the infidels and heretics from other countries. There are few choices, and we must begin the search now."

The tsar was correct about Snow faking her illness, just as she apparently had during her father's wedding. When five days had passed and no one reported any activity from her, His Majesty ordered an imperial physician to examine her.

This is when the entire court discovered Snow was absent from her bedchamber despite servants regularly having delivered meals to her door and collecting empty trays placed outside. Two of her most trusted ladies usually posted outside her chambers could not or would not account for the tsarevna's absence.

"She is gone, and no one knows where," the royal physician had the unenviable task of reporting to her father and grandfather.

"Gone where? How?" the tsar thundered.

"When?" Alex demanded, and all of her ladies were summoned one by one to his chambers for what amounted to an interrogation.

None knew. Or perhaps none would report on their mistress. This seemed odd, as normally each of them appeared terrified of Snow.

Tatiana did not fear foul play. It would be just like Snow to stage her own disappearance. She loved drama, and to be the center of attention. Tatiana knew Alexander would agonize about the girl's absence—that somehow Snow had found the one method of ensuring that the entire kingdom's attention would shift to her and all would be in an uproar if she didn't return.

Alexander was devastated. "Send out the tsar's army and all of my men. Scatter them throughout the kingdom and spare no man and no expense until my daughter is found!"

The armies thundered out of the Kremlin.

It was an alarming spring.

Chapter 16

Bells chimed for any and all occasions, including holidays, religious observances, celebrations, death knells, important marriages or births, war dangers or victories, and fires. Today no one had ever heard Moskva's bells clang so loudly and ferociously. They rang to summon all the townsfolk and the soldiers to search for the missing princess. Since the hundreds, even thousands of bells in all sizes and timbres fashioned from copper, bronze, iron, and silver occupied every bell tower and laddered niche, the noise deafened the court and the city. It reverberated day and night, and there was not a soul in the surrounding countryside who did not know that Princess Snowdrop was missing from the palace. Commoners fought over who would get to pull on the closest bell ropes or they joined in the hunt.

"I fear she is dead," Alex said forlornly after an entire week had passed. Tatiana had convinced Alex to rest and take the afternoon nap with her after he had spent all that time away searching on horseback as far as Yaroslavl.

"I don't believe that," she reassured him. "It's just that there are so many places to look in such a huge city. Not to mention a massive country thick with towns and country-side."

He could not sleep, any more than he had been able to since Snow's disappearance had been discovered. Again and again Tatiana tried to convince Alex that his daughter had chosen to leave rather than been kidnapped. He refused to believe it.

"I think we should threaten Snow's two ladies more force-fully," she suggested now. "Surely they know something or saw something. It is possible she was gone for days and days before we learned of it."

"Both ladies are missing now, too," he said grimly. "And Tanya, she had no reason to leave. I gave her everything!"

Except your time, Tatiana thought bleakly. *And her free-dom.*

The grand duchess had been raised in the terem, yet surely she must long to see more of the outside world, as her step-mother did. Both existed like doves in giant gilded cages, and so why wouldn't Snow have tried to get away when presented with a passageway enabling her to do just that?

She could not, however, bring herself to tell Alex about the other tunnel. He might be more infuriated by her fail-ure to tell him that than anything, as evidenced when he had checked the passageway behind the unicorn and found the same layers of dust she had. "No one could have taken her from here," he mused when he saw the dust. "God's teeth, I will kill the bastard who did! I just cannot imagine how it happened."

Another week passed, with seemingly the entire tsardom searching in vain.

Convinced she had to do something, even if it meant telling Alex and the tsar about the huntsman Igor, who could perhaps be located, she decided to turn to the magic mirror. She had little faith it would reveal anything, though, since she herself needed no protection from harm.

To her surprise, as soon as she had locked herself in her bedchamber and pulled out the amber and pewter mirror by its elaborate handle, a strong melodious voice immediately issued forth:

> *Seek out Baba's hut if you dare*
> *For help finding the one most fair.*
> *The pale princess with the golden hair*
> *dwells with seven in a forest lair.*

She shook the mirror again, placed it back down and then picked it back up. It did not repeat itself.

With seven? In a lair? In the *forest*? How was any of this possible? And she was to meet Baba Yaga once again? Here? And how?

***

The plan was elaborate, not to mention dangerous. And it entailed first and foremost confessing her encounters with Baba Yaga to her bogatyr cousins. Would they even believe her?

She had to enlist help from Olga and Sonya, as well. She saw no way to gain their cooperation without telling them, too, all about what had happened in the forest nearly two years ago.

She chose a bench in the gardens again, since the castle was riddled with spy holes in the walls and alcoves where anyone could overhear.

Olga believed her immediately. "And so that is how His Lordship your father was actually healed?"

As Tatiana nodded, she noticed Sonya surreptitiously cross herself. "It is not possible," she murmured.

So Tatiana showed them the mirror, which now remained silent. She also explained how she had gained possession of the vial of poison antidote.

Sonya began to believe; however, she did not hesitate to voice her concerns over Tatiana's plan to flee to the forest and search for Snow. "How do you know this witch can, as you say, help you? Or that she would?"

"My mother gave me good advice about her before she died. She told me if I were kind to Baba Yaga, she would be kind to me, as well." She showed them the little matryoshka her mother had left her. "And this has served as her blessing all these years."

"Baba Yaga, though? Isn't she a cannibal?"

"Only in legends, I believe. She's more of a grandmother than a witch. A Wise Woman, even."

"Still—"

"It happened, my Sonya. You have seen the vial and the mirror. You saw my beloved father recover suddenly. I cannot devote any more time to convincing you Baba Yaga is real."

"It's not that I don't believe she exists . . ."

"You don't have to accept this as truth. Just help me get to her—or into the forest where I believe she and her hut stand now."

"I will help you," Olga said quietly. "I believe everything you told us and I have known you since you were a babe. You do not lie."

"Except to sneak into the forest from Tolkov," Sonya said wryly.

"You knew?"

"Everybody did," Olga and Sonya said simultaneously.

The three broke out laughing.

"I wouldn't be surprised if my father knew, too." He certainly had hinted that he did.

"Most likely. Now, let us plan," Sonya urged briskly, and Tatiana was relieved her former tutor would assist.

In the days to come, Tatiana arranged to meet with all three knights just inside the tunnel behind the rose trellis. Olga explained to them how to enter, and each took turns slipping in surreptitiously.

Huddled in the mouth of the tunnel, Mikhail and Igor did not believe her at first. It took a lot of persuasion from Sir Dimitri to convince them that not only was Tatiana conversant with forest life and with a famous witch, but that she actually had a destination—or two.

"Your father, let alone your husband, would never agree

to such an absurd and deadly plan!" Igor protested the most, pulling anxiously on his long gray beard. "And our heads will be mounted on the walls of Tolkov Castle if anything goes wrong, if not on the Kremlin towers."

"Which is exactly why I need your assistance. My scheme has a much better chance of success if I am protected by three armed bogatyrs than if I go alone."

"And she would," Sir Mikhail pronounced grimly. "Go alone."

Of that there was no doubt.

*****

Tatiana would dress this time as a huntsman, complete with bow, quiver of arrows, and a horse. As a fourth horseman with three heavily armed knights, she would blend in and be safe. Her only concern was that she might not locate Baba Yaga's hut in the company of three men.

She would leave a note for Alex and follow the exit in his apartments. No matter where on the river bank it ended, it was less risky than emerging in a huntsman's outfit in the middle of a rose garden attended by mostly noble ladies—and much easier than slipping into Snow's bedchamber where that particular passage started.

From the river she would meet the others in the royal stables.

She left the note somewhere Alex would find it, albeit not too soon: atop the pile of urgent petitions that he barely handled right now:

My Dearest, I have gone in search of Snow myself because I believe I may be the only one who can locate her. Do not search for me if you wish me to succeed. Rest assured that I have taken precautions to ensure my safety.

Your loving wife.

With Olga and Sonya covering for her much the way Snow's ladies had done—pretending to go in and out of her bedchamber to attend her—if she were fortunate, no one would miss her for several days.

It was easy to smuggle clothing into Alex's apartment, along with the small sack she had once carried everywhere, now again containing the vial, the mirror, and her mother's doll.

As soon as she had pushed the button behind the unicorn and pulled the door shut behind herself, she found that the cobwebs were indeed thick. Thankfully Olga had trimmed Tatiana's lovely hair short enough for it to fit under a tall fur hat. Her lack of a beard simply would mark her as a boy apprentice.

The floor sloped downward most of the way. Fortunately, she had brought a lighted rush with her for the sconces she believed must be there. They were.

It took awhile to reach the first of what would be four iron doors. Fortunately, each was propped open enough for her to slide through. When she spied the unused locks, however, she shuddered to realize how close she might have come to being trapped down here until she died.

There was little light to tell her she had reached the end,

so when she pulled open the fourth door, she nearly crashed into a tall fir tree.

It was a perfect disguise for the door leading back to the tunnel, and she suspected she would be able to return via the same route. After all, if she found Snow, the girl already knew about this exit.

Hiding beneath the lower boughs, Tatiana watched barges and boats sailing the river. It was now late spring, the water still containing chunks of ice that forced all the vessels to pole around them, and thus the boatmen's attention was not on the shore where she hid. She also peered across the river and down both sides of the bank so she could memorize the exact location of the entrance.

She made her way swiftly onto the riverbank, immediately striding along as if she had been walking this bank for a long time. When no one yelled to her, she felt assured that none of the vessel crews had noticed a huntsman suddenly emerge from a tree. If they did, perhaps they had assumed a man might step behind a tree because he needed to make water.

With so many outbuildings and annexes in the Kremlin and its squares, it took her awhile to locate the stables. Fortunately it was only a half hour after the designated meeting time.

Seeing her arrive, at first her father's knights did not recognize her. She tried out her new and intentionally gruff voice on them. "Let's go, men."

Dimitri's eyes opened wide. The other two bogatyrs stared at her blankly from the barrels where they sat.

"Yes, we should depart immediately," Dimitri agreed, and motioned to Igor and Mikhail to bring the horses.

It was early afternoon and exceptionally warm for a spring day. Tatiana, regardless of the seriousness of their venture, could barely contain her excitement as she mounted a bay gelding and urged it to follow the other horses.

They made it to the forest in what seemed like minutes, and Tatiana took deep breaths as her surroundings closed in on them. Larks and thrushes pealed out their songs, the grass served as cover for a dozen varieties of wildflowers, and squirrels and chipmunks scattered across the path into the brush. She felt happier than she had in months, and suffered no guilt for it.

The men had agreed with her suggestion that they trot or walk the horses most of the time, with the intent of not scaring off anyone or anything. Tatiana assumed they would need to find clearings similar to the one where Baba Yaga had landed her hut outside Tolkov.

Three days passed, with the four of them camping each evening in tents made from linen and canvas sails. It was almost as it had been two summers ago when they had escorted her to Moskva. Yet this was a very different journey, with a very different purpose.

Tatiana prayed morning and night that they would succeed—and quickly.

Chapter 17

At times the foursome gathered in a designated place before each rode slowly in a different direction and then regrouped later. Thus far they'd encountered only a few of Alex's men (who appeared too calm to know their lord was missing a wife as well as a daughter), so it was relatively easy to search uninterrupted.

Late on the fourth afternoon Tatiana was riding straight north when she imagined she heard the familiar cackle of a giant chicken. She pulled on the reins and listened again before edging the horse slowly toward a clearing barely visible between the stick-like birches with papery bark that smeared the forest with a pink glow.

There it was. The hut had its back to the clearing, with

Baba Yaga's cauldron-like travel vessel leaned against a fence post topped with a worn skull.

She dismounted and led her horse the rest of the way, deciding it was too risky to go back and get the others. What if she couldn't find the hut again? What if Baba refused to admit three middle-aged men to her domain?

The horse whinnied with nervousness until she hobbled him in a patch of lime bright grass near the cauldron. If the others came along, they would know she was there.

Trim and colorful in her royal blue huntsman's kaftan, she removed her lynx-fur hat and shook her shorter hair to fluff it about. Even though the magic mirror had sent her, that was no guarantee Baba would welcome—let alone remember—her. At least she would find out in moments if the hut itself would accommodate her:

Little hut, little hut! Turn your back to the forest and your front to me!

The hut lifted immediately, twirling with fewer creaks and screeches than she remembered. In fact, the staircase dropped from the doorway to the chicken's widespread feet rapidly, and Tatiana felt her nervousness dissipate.

She was welcome—or perhaps expected.

Both appeared to be true, as Baba opened the door and beckoned her inside.

The witch looked as she remembered. Only her silver locks seemed to have grown over the fat bosom that clashed incongruously with her bony frame. Now her hair reached all the way to her waist. She smoked a pipe and wore a red sarafan embroidered with the mythical firebird.

The hut appeared much larger this time, too, with two cots rather than one and two pans bubbling on the huge stove.

"Did you bring your mother's blessing?"

"My what? Oh, yes I did." Tatiana reached into the pouch hanging on her shoulder and started to remove the small nested doll.

"No matter," Baba said gruffly. "I will help you either way."

"How do you know that I need help? Did the mirror tell you?"

"Child—young lady—I told you once before that I know your future. I sensed that you would be back here in this exact forest after you left me with the mirror. I take it you found the looking glass's advice useful?"

"It led me here. I'm trying to locate someone who is in these woods—according to the looking glass."

"Of course." The witch waved her into a chair and retreated to the stove to stir something.

She then settled herself into a chair opposite Tatiana, much as she had on the two previous visits. "She is here."

"She is? With you?"

"*Nyet!* I do not assist those with evil in their hearts."

"Is she well?"

"Oh yes. Very well, I should venture."

"Where exactly is she?"

"With the leshi."

"Who?" The word seemed familiar. Tatiana could not recall why.

"The leshi are the forest spirits. Surely your education taught you this."

"I forgot about them. And I have never encountered a supernatural being in the forest—not in Tolkov and not here so far. Besides yourself," she added shyly.

"They dwell in places that most humans would not be able to see." Baba took several puffs on her pipe.

It appeared Tatiana would have to drag the information out of the witch, who seemed to be enjoying herself. "Then how will I locate her? The mirror told me she is in their lair."

"You shall have assistance, of course. I have arranged for you to meet one of them."

"When?"

"Not so quickly. First we shall dine, then have tea, and then you must tell me stories of life at the Kremlin where the richest of humans dwell."

"I shall need to inform my traveling companions of my whereabouts. They know I am looking for you," she added as Baba frowned.

"No fears. I have sent them on an impossible chase else-where. They will be away for days. And I believe the leshi do not wish to be located, either, so they have little hope of discovering anything until it is willed thus."

"But—"

"Are you hungry for my stew or not?"

As she nodded, Tatiana heard the unmistakable sound of the ladder retreating up into the hut's door. Obviously there would be no escape unless she wished to jump the equivalent of two stories.

With a sigh, she moved over to the table with Baba, who

fed her a heaping bowl of rabbit stew, a loaf of black bread, and cherry tarts.

"Have no fear," Baba said after Tatiana had recounted the story of Snowdrop and her escape from the terem. She then motioned to the second cot, covered with a warm quilt. There would be no campsite on the hard forest floor tonight.

"Remember," Baba told her as they both climbed into their beds. "Morning is wiser than the evening."

***

After dawn Baba gave her directions for breaking their fast, and if she weren't so worried about reactions to her own disappearance (for surely by now her absence had been discovered at the Kremlin) she might have enjoyed herself. She had not been in a kitchen in a couple years now, and Baba's cupboards were heaped with delightful food stuffs and filled with the smells of simmering herbs and spices.

Now she produced warm bread slathered with peach preserves, boiled duck eggs, and porridge. "You could stay and keep house for me," Baba grinned, her iron teeth gleaming in the sunlight filtering through the hut window. "I have no problem with you living here."

"I could," she smiled back, not worried that the witch was serious. "Usually I'm a poor cleaner and cook. And I'm worse at stitching," she added, pointing to the bolts of cloth and half-finished embroideries in one corner near the loom.

"Ah, but you know plants. I can always use assistance with pounding herbs, making poultices, and grinding plants into liquids." The witch said this absentmindedly, tapping her extremely long, talon-like fingernails on the table where they ate.

"I must first find the tsarevna."

"Indeed. Princesses should not live in the forest with the spirits. They upset nature's balance."

"Is it far? Where Snow lives?"

"Ah, I cannot give out such information. That is up to the leshi. Not even I may see their lair unless they decide I should."

"Then must I convince them to take me to her?"

Baba stood and began taking down some of the plants hanging overhead in the sunlight. "I will give you some help—not with the leshi. They will seek you themselves, as I advised them you might be arriving. If you desire to retrieve this evil princess—and I fail to see why you would—you will need my assistance."

"Thank you, Grandmother."

"Take this." Out of her cupboard she had pulled a delicate hair comb glittering with tiny garnets and emeralds. "The girl is vain, is she not? She told the leshi she was the most 'fair' in Rus, albeit she must have neglected to mention you."

Surprised and honored, Tatiana thanked Baba and started to slip the comb into her pouch.

"Not yet! I must first dip it in one of my potions. If you can affix it to her hair, she will fall asleep as long as it remains there. This should give your precious knights time to bring her back to Moskva."

"I know not how to locate the leshi."

"They will find you when they find you. But look carefully. They can shape shift at any time, going from as large as a tall pine to as short as a mushroom. In fact, they can appear *as* mushrooms, which is why you will never find them if they don't wish it."

"Thank you, Grandmother." She watched as Baba dipped the comb in some lotion that dried instantly, then wrapped the comb in a fancy cloth bag before handing it to Tatiana.

"Now, we must alter your appearance a bit more." Baba reached into yet another cupboard and brought out a tall glass beaker. "This is brown dye. I gather larch and pine needles in the autumn, and always mix them with walnut husks. This will keep your skin that color for weeks if you need it." She shook a bit on a cloth and rubbed it carefully on Tatiana's face and neck.

"Thank you. That might help my disguise, as I fear she will not accept anything from me if I am recognized."

"That is why you need this," Baba said, pulling a darker brown hunk of lamb's wool out of the same cupboard and signaling to Tatiana while she pasted it on her chin. "Now you have a beard like all the other men."

"And if I fail?"

"Will you?"

"I don't think so," Tatiana answered confidently.

"Come back to me if she refuses the comb. Off with you then." She opened the door and Tatiana realized that the ladder had been lowered some time while they slept.

Before she could ask any more questions, Baba had given her a nudge forward.

Clambering easily down the wooden stairs, Tatiana felt brave and bold. She would seek the leshi first, then find

Snow, then find the bogatyrs. Somehow it all seemed manageable now.

**

The man stood at the opposite side of the clearing. She would not know he was a man at all if she hadn't been watching for oddities in the forest and spotted what appeared to be a red scarf wrapped around a birch. Indeed, he resembled nothing so much as a tree, with his beard and hair fashioned from roots and grasses. His entire body could have been the leafy branches of a cottonwood, decorated with moss, pinecones, and bark. His face, cheeks, and lips, just visible above a hint of peasant attire, glowed with a touch of blue.

"Your Imperial Highness," he greeted her, though she was the one who bowed to him.

"I await your command," she said politely, finding herself almost within touching distance of the spirit.

"It will be a pleasure to assist you. Much good news of your care of our forests reaches our ears, and we are grateful that you have served as such a good caretaker of the land."

"I love the forest," she said earnestly. "I would normally enjoy my time here much more if I were not seeking a runaway princess."

"This we know. Or at least the leshi are aware of your presence here. The girl is not. She is hardly a girl, however." Tatiana thought one bright green eye closed in a wink.

"She is with you?"

"With my six brothers who protect the forest and all the wildlife within it."

"Then she is helping you?"

"Not particularly. She does tidy up our home a bit half-heartedly. Other than that we find her a nuisance. An annoying and slightly shrill one, to be specific."

"And you will take me to her?"

"Only if you promise not to share our location with anyone. That includes the three knights who are currently riding in circles trying to locate you." Now he laughed. "This was one of my favorite tricks yesterday. I have rearranged all the signposts so that no matter which one they follow, they will arrive back where they commenced their search."

Tatiana wanted to chuckle at the thought of Igor, Mikhail, and Dimitri desperately circling the forest and finding all of their usual scouting and patrolling skills of no avail. Yet she did feel a prick of conscience at how worried they must be.

"The princess has warned us not to open the door to any soldiers. *You* should not raise any suspicions," he told her as they began to enter a more heavily wooded area.

Within minutes they had arrived at what must surely be the lair of the leshi. The enormous oak tree with a door carved into the bark surely hadn't been here previously—at least not in its current form. When she turned back to ask her companion if its size had been altered recently, he had vanished.

Just as she prepared to approach the door, it opened. Stepping quickly behind a recently budded forsythia bush, Tatiana watched in amazement as Snowdrop came outside carrying an empty basket.

She was not shocked that the grand duchess was here. Nor was she surprised that the girl wore peasant clothing. Nor did it amaze her that Snow had obviously dyed her hair black as ebony, emphasizing her pale skin, which now appeared as soft and clear as a pure white rose.

Yet Tatiana was stunned and shaken. Without the bulky sarafan she usually wore, it was immediately obvious that Snow was undeniably pregnant!

Chapter 18

The entire tsardom would be scandalized, Tatiana realized instantly. Perhaps here, then, was the explanation for Snow's flight from the Kremlin and her father, not to mention her unnaturally glowing skin earlier last summer.

Allowing herself to follow the girl, she made enough noise that Snow would know someone else was present and not be terrified of a stranger.

"*Devushka*! Young lady!" Tatiana cried, forcing her deepest voice to take on a hint of desperation.

The girl pivoted, pausing in the process of picking dandelions and daisies. "What do you want?" Rather than frightened, she seemed annoyed.

"I seek only some bread for my daily meal," Tatiana said,

concentrating on keeping her voice low. "And here, I have something to pay for it."

Curious, Snow moved toward her. Tatiana held up the comb toward the sun so that the gems sparkled from afar.

"It's pretty enough, I suppose."

Spoken like a spoiled princess, Tatiana thought. "It is yours for a loaf of bread."

"An entire loaf? I don't believe so." She started to turn away.

"Just a hunk of bread perhaps?"

"Very well." She reached out for the comb. Tatiana, anticipating that this might not work if she didn't wait for the bread first, held it above Snow's head.

"Wait here," Snow commanded. "I will give you a piece of bread, for that's all the bauble is worth."

Tatiana desperately wanted to follow her inside the oak tree home without scaring the girl. She waited a few moments until Snow returned. After making the trade, she hesitated. How would she ensure that the comb was inserted into her hair?

"Would you like to try it on?" she urged. "It belonged to my mother, and I'd like to see how it looks in a woman's hair for the last time."

When Snow hesitated, she added, "Or perhaps you would like your husband to be the first to admire it?"

Carelessly Snow pushed the comb into her hair. "He is dead. He was a huntsman like you, which is why I humor you. Now good day."

She turned and carried her basket back into the house once

again, leaving Tatiana surprised, sad, and uncertain what to do next.

She decided to hide behind the bush again. If no one came along, she would sneak inside and ensure that Snow was indeed asleep. Presumably, according to Baba Yaga and the leshi spirit, her father's knights would encounter her shortly and they could transport the princess back to the Kremlin.

She had no idea how to move a woman so obviously ready to give birth, let alone how they would begin to explain it all to Alex and the tsar.

***

Unfortunately, the only ones who came along were what appeared to be six additional leshi. At least she thought that's who they were, as the figures sauntering in her direction resembled thick moving branches no higher than her own waist. Thinner limbs served as legs and arms, and their faces were barely visible beneath bushy grass beards and mustaches.

Within minutes of entering the tree, however, one of them reopened the door and tossed out something that glittered as it fell to the forest floor. The comb! Now it would never work.

"She must have allowed a soldier to enter," a voice squeaked.

"Alas, she will be fine," another replied. "At least we could have gotten some reprieve from that sword-sharp tongue of hers."

The door closed again, blocking the noise, and Tatiana

stood feeling dejected. She could not save Snow—or her innocent baby.

Remembering Baba's invitation to return to her if she failed, she trudged back the way she had come, unsurprised when she easily encountered the hut standing proudly on its fowl legs.

She almost didn't notice that two goats were tied out beside her own horse, which had apparently been fed and brushed and looked contently at her. All three animals were now securely pastured within a large bone fence similar to the one Baba had had in Tolkov forest. Perhaps she intended to stay here awhile, too.

Relieved, Tatiana rapped on the door until the witch responded.

"I feared the leshi might interfere," Baba said at once. "Although they delight in playing tricks on humans, I presumed they would want to rid themselves of your princess, not rescue her."

"She's pregnant!" Tatiana blurted out. "By my calculations, she is nearly ready to deliver the babe!"

"Of course," Baba said mildly, and waved to another corner. The inside of the hut seemed to have expanded yet again, and this time it accommodated a third bed and a cradle!

"For Snow's baby?"

"In case it is needed."

"I thought you detested children."

"Rumors to keep the little ones from bothering me day and night, nothing more."

"And the skulls?" she asked a bit nervously.

"Few are human. And yes, in answer to your next query, I

have had my own children. Two daughters who died before they turned twenty years. No grandchildren."

"I'm sorry," Tatiana stammered. "I didn't know."

"Secrets are meant to be kept, *da*?"

Tatiana felt herself blush. "I *did* reveal yours—I mean, I told two of my ladies and the three knights with me that I had met you."

Baba waved a hand in dismissal. "Sometimes secrets must be revealed to unveil or protect larger secrets. Or to reveal oneself to a loved one."

She beckoned to the table, set with roast hare and watermelon slices, cheese- and meat-filled dumplings, and glasses of kvass.

"Let us eat and rest, Tanya. We will find a new plan."

As they curled into their respective cots a bit later, Baba seemed to sense the questions and problems whirling around in her guest's mind. "Remember," she whispered in the dark. "Morning is wiser than the evening."

Three days passed.

Baba assured Tatiana it was much too early to try so soon to trick Snow again.

"For this attempt," Baba said when they broke their fast on the fourth day, "I must go. Your disguise will not work a second time. And that baby must be due to arrive any day."

Tatiana noticed that Baba had taken on a slightly different appearance. She now resembled a peasant woman, complete with a floral scarf such as old babushkas wore.

"I've calculated the months that have passed since we sent away the presumed father—one of the tsar's huntsmen. She should be delivered of a child any day," Tatiana told Baba.

"I will pose as a midwife. Surely the leshi cannot manage on their own."

"Thank you, Grandmother. Should I follow in case I am needed as well?"

"No. I have performed such duties before."

Then Baba extracted a glass bottle filled with a yellow liquid from her apron. "This potion will give her back her strength and health after the babe is born. It will also cause her to sleep for endless hours."

"So that we will be able to bring her back to the palace?"

"If she so chooses. I shall not return until the baby arrives, so work on grinding some dandelion greens into a curative should there be any problems after the birthing."

***

Another three days passed. And then three more. Tatiana passed her time pounding herbs and extracting sap from balsam fir branches she gathered outside. The sap could be used in a poultice to treat wounds, so presumably both she and Baba could benefit from the supply. She also located some cattails Baba had apparently gathered by the nearby stream, and used their roots to concoct a salve for burns.

In those agonizing days of waiting, she realized how much she was worried about Alex and his response to her flight. She could only imagine how he must have reacted to her note, which hopefully he had found.

She also realized something else: she had managed to fall completely in love with her husband at long last. Always before she had held back a little of herself, and now she resolved to tell him everything. She would confess all her forbidden forest trips, tell him about Baba Yaga, and give him the sad truth about Snowdrop. There must be no more secrets if they were to be totally happy—even if those revelations destroyed their relationship.

When Baba did arrive, she was not alone. Nor was Snow with her.

She did carry with her a small bundle wrapped in a blanket.

Chapter 19

Why do you have the grand duchess's child? Assuming that is what is wrapped in the blanket?"

Baba set the bundle carefully in the cradle and unswaddled some of the cloth. A pair of wide-open, forget-me-not blue eyes stared up at both of them.

"She didn't want her," Baba said simply, settling heavily on her chair.

"My God. Let me make you some birch tea."

"Thank you, dearest Tanya. These days have been difficult. I offered to allow the leshi to keep the infant—a half-hearted offer at best. They declined anyway."

"What is wrong with Snowdrop? Why would she not desire to keep the child and raise it? Maybe not in the forest, but perhaps in the palace. Did she say she was afraid to go home?"

Baba waved her arm as if whisking away bad thoughts. "She speaks little. When she does, she barks orders like a dog. The leshi detest her and want her gone, and she claims she has no interest in being a mother."

"I never thought . . . well, I assumed after losing her own mother at a young age she would want a family again."

Baba looked as if she had the weight of the world on her narrow, slumped shoulders. "I think she helped that along."

"What do you mean?"

"Her mother's death. None of the women I secretly sent to treat your husband's first wife, Grand Duchess Natalya Sergeievna, could figure out her illness or a cure. Separately they all told me it might be poison. We knew she and her husband did not get along, yet he is a good man. Nearly all of the healers suspected the rude little grand duchess who barely visited."

"Why would she do such a thing?"

"Perhaps to prevent her own mother from bearing another child. Thus bringing her closer to the throne. I don't know."

Tatiana immediately recalled what had happened to herself on the night of Snow's birthday. "I meant to tell you earlier, Grandmother. I injected the drops from the vial you gave me two years ago when I became with child and nearly died."

"I know, *devushka*, I know it well. I foresaw that when I met you, which is why I gave you both that and the looking glass, which you already told me was of great assistance. If I read her motives correctly, the idea of you as a pregnant step-mother who might give birth to a male heir was not something the princess would have accepted."

"But she is a *woman.* She cannot ascend the Russian throne, not unless it is a small principality like my father rules. And technically she's a grand duchess, not a princess."

"I don't know. Yet if you have no child, her own child— when it is not a bastard child like this one is—would be next in line for the throne after her father."

"Alex! Do you think he's in danger?"

"Not with her hidden away in the tree home, and certainly not until he arranges a royal marriage for her."

"She is adamant about not getting married, though! Well, at least she was. Then again—"

"Indeed. Then she was pregnant by a commoner. Now that impediment is gone—and that impediment needs some goat's milk!"

They continued to talk through the situation while dipping a cloth in a bowl of milk and alternating holding it for the baby to suck. It would not be easy keeping the tiny thing alive; Snow had, according to Baba, permitted it to breastfeed for the first couple days after childbirth.

"I will find us a townswoman who is nursing a baby and can help," Baba decided. "I could send you. However, I think I might be more persuasive." She winked, and albeit sad about the baby's predicament, Tatiana laughed.

"That might be true, especially since right now I resemble a short-haired, bearded huntsman with dark skin." As she worked off the glue that held the beard to her chin, she thought about sirs Dimitri, Mikhail, and Igor. Did the leshi still have them circling the forest in a non-ending spiral?

As if reading her thoughts, Baba Yaga said, "You will be safer remaining with me for now, my dear. We need to wait and watch to see if Snow returns to the palace. If so, you may return, as well; otherwise, we must continue to attempt to convince her to return. Or force her to do so."

"You said the potion you brought her not only would strengthen her, but also put her to sleep frequently!"

"She grabbed that bottle from me and threw it across the room before I could stop her. It smashed on the hearth."

Baba's eyes narrowed in what Tatiana suspected was suppressed fury. "When that failed, I waited for her to nap and then left her a shawl of French lace I knew she would be unable to resist. I hung it on the bedpost, knowing that when she wore it she would sleep for so many hours we could then get your bogatyrs to take her home before she awoke."

"So the problem is actually solved?"

"*Nyet!*" Baba's eyes blazed with anger. "One of the leshi came home before she awoke and saw it. He sniffed the lace and then tossed the entire shawl in the hearth where it burned instantly."

Baba stared down at the cradle and Tatiana wasn't certain if she imagined seeing a teardrop running down one of the old witch's cheeks.

"When she awakened and again told me, 'Get rid of that thing,' I took the child and left. No one stopped me," she added, her pointed jaw tightening.

Now Tatiana was furious, as well. She picked up the child, who apparently had had enough milk and now gurgled a bit. Soon the baby slept, only after Baba taught Tatiana how to get her to burp before returning her to the cradle.

Before Baba left, Tatiana scribbled a hasty note that could be delivered to Alex now:

My dearest. I am fine and safe. Snow is alive and well. I will work on returning her to the castle as soon as it is possible to do so. Please do not share this information with anyone, perhaps not even the tsar unless you think it is essential.

All love, Tanya.

In a few minutes Tatiana heard the cauldron *whoosh* on its liftoff and looked out to see it moving swiftly across the emerald treetops as Baba steered with the mortar, taking her closer to the city. And hopefully a nursing mother.

***

True to her word, Baba returned in a few hours with a plump young woman who appeared only slightly nervous about Baba Yaga after she was handed the baby.

"Kristina lost her own babe only a week ago," Baba explained, and the two watched as the woman immediately settled into Baba's rocker and pulled open her thin gown to reveal breasts swollen with milk. The baby sucked hungrily, and both Tatiana and Baba breathed concurrent sighs of relief.

At night Kristina slept restlessly on the third cot, rising almost hourly to breastfeed the child. "May I call her Olga?" she asked shyly after a couple days. "It was to be my own babe's name." She crossed herself with her right hand while comfortably balancing the child on her left arm.

As much as Tatiana admired the child and enjoyed holding her, she had determined that regardless of Snow's continued presence in the forest, she herself must return home. She had taken note of Baba's revelation that the healers she sent believed that Alex and Natalya never got along, and admitted to herself that she found this news welcome. Now she must go back to him. To the palace. To her life as the tsarevna.

Baba concurred, seeming less reluctant than she might have been if she hadn't gained another guest—or two. "*Da*, I agree. We at least must make a third attempt to induce her to return or ensure she sleeps while escorted to the Kremlin. Tanya, you must go yourself this time. She will recognize me unless I appear to her in my younger guise, which inevitably will make her feel jealous and treat me as a potential rival."

"She knows me, too!"

"She knows you as your young and fair self and also as a handsome huntsman. She does not," Baba winked, "know you as a helpful and generous crone who poses no threat."

"She refused your potion and the leshi discovered the power of the lace."

"No matter. I can transform you into exactly what you might look like sixty years from now—just a more impoverished version. And there will be no need for you to approach her too closely.

"Go ahead," Baba urged. "See what the mirror tells you, too."

Tatiana slipped the looking glass out of her sack and waited a few moments before it spoke:

> *If you can convince her that you care*
> *You need do little to prepare.*
> *The golden apple you should bear*
> *Will attract the girl with ebony hair.*

"Goodness, the mirror even knows that Snow dyed her hair!" Tatiana said in surprise.

"Hmm. And I think I know what apple the mirror mentions," Baba added thoughtfully.

"All I know is that apples are her favorite fruit and that she adores jewelry. Does that help?"

"According to the looking glass, that's all you need. That and to gain her trust."

"Perhaps I could bring her news of the baby."

"That might work—if she has any interest in the child," Baba said wryly.

Kristina, rocking baby Olga as usual, had overheard. "Are you bringing the baby back to the awful woman who abandoned her?"

"We will offer her one more opportunity," Baba said firmly. "However, if she is uninterested . . ." She stared thoughtfully at Kristina.

"My husband and I would raise her well, Grandmother. I can assure you of that. We have waited so many years for a child, and then to lose ours . . . well, my husband is as devastated as I am."

"This," Baba said, "we will certainly take into consideration." Tatiana nodded then frowned. Could they really give away a royal child to a peasant couple? Would anyone protest? Was it fair to the child? What if Snowdrop changed her mind?

As if reading her thoughts, Baba reached out a hand to Tatiana. "All will be as it should. You will know the answers to your reservations and questions tomorrow."

"And the locket that you are holding?"

Baba held the gold locket up to the light. "This will work, I assure you. Tonight I shall fashion it and in the morning you shall deliver it. Now have some tea and get some sleep."

"I know," Tatiana grinned. "Morning is wiser than the evening."

Chapter 20

As an opalescent dawn breached the clearing, Baba Yaga showed her handiwork to Kristina—whom she seemed to trust—and Tatiana.

The locket fell below the neckline. Its chain ended in a miniature golden apple, complete with an emerald stem and a circlet of tiny garnets around the fruit.

"Make certain you advise the grand duchess to keep it hidden beneath her sarafan at all times," Baba warned.

"Why? Won't she want to show it off?"

"Perhaps, although once she puts it on, she will be in no condition to make such adjustments to her wardrobe."

"I see. So it is powerful?"

"Extremely."

"In what way?"

"This you—and Snow—will learn."

"Will it harm her—or just put her to sleep?"

"No harm shall come to the young princess. Certainly less harm than if she continues to haunt the leshi and these forestlands."

Relieved, Tatiana waited patiently while Baba began to effect the transformation from her young self into an apparently helpful and generous crone. This involved much magic, of which Tatiana was of course ignorant. She knew only that her smooth hands with the pearly fingernails soon turned wrinkled and coarse.

She carefully dressed in a tattered orange sarafan with loose threads, as well as an equally worn yet sturdy pair of boots. Her now short hair was pinned up loosely on her head, and then Baba draped a tangerine scarf patterned with faded lilies around her head and shoulders. At first she dared not gaze at herself in the mirror, as Baba had given her a special potion to drink.

"It will wear off in one day," Baba assured her as Tatiana gasped.

She resembled a softer version of Baba, with accordion-like wrinkles on her cheeks and faint brown spots on her chin and forehead. The bits of hair poking out of the top of the scarf appeared silver.

"Your voice will be weaker now," Baba advised. "That, too, shall change back in a half a day's time."

"So should I return to you when I have finished my task?" she asked hopefully.

"There will be no need if you succeed. And your knights will return you to your palace within two days' time. Kristina and the baby shall stay with me for now unless you send word with one of the leshi that the baby should be brought to the palace."

"Will I see you again?"

"Time will tell, my sweet Tanya. Rest assured that the forests of the tsardom are my home, and you shall always be able to find me when and if you need me."

Suddenly Tatiana felt like crying. Baba had become like a mother rather than a grandmother to her, and she could not bear the thought of never seeing her again.

"I have a gift for you—actually two," Baba said. She pulled out a golden chain that resembled the one Tatiana would present to Snow, but from which dangled something entirely different than the apple.

"What is it?" Tatiana asked in awe.

The gleaming, glass-like piece appeared black as Snow's hair and dotted with sparkling white crystals that resembled snowflakes.

"It is snowflake obsidian. Wear it beneath your clothing so you have it with you at all times when you are in Snow's presence. After she awakens, that is."

"Why?"

"It has several powers, the most extraordinary being that it can freeze anything hot in a moment's time."

"Why should I need such a thing? It is simply beautiful, though," she hastened to add.

"It is formed from volcanic lava when it rapidly cools—hence its remarkable power. It also possesses a soothing and calming influence."

"I don't see—"

"You will," she assured her in a gruff voice. "Just wear it, though not necessarily now."

"Thank you, Grandmother. For all you have done for me." She wrapped the snowflake obsidian necklace in cloth and carefully placed it into her sack.

"Here," Baba said more softly, handing her something else. "Put this, too, in the sack with the vial, which we pray you will never need, and the looking glass in case you ever need advice in a dangerous situation. This, however, is *my* blessing."

Tatiana could barely see it through her tears: a tiny matryoshka doll with a painted likeness of Baba's hut on chicken legs on the outside doll.

"Inside you will find a slightly smaller doll with a painting of me, then my mortar and then cauldron nested in subsequent dolls. You always have had your mother's blessing, and now you have mine."

They hugged for what might or might not be the last time.

Still teary-eyed, Tatiana gathered up what little she had or needed and wished Kristina well.

The ladder dropped for her, and outside she decided to saddle the horse on which she had arrived. Perhaps Snow would think it odd that such a poor and decrepit old woman possessed such a fine horse, so she would tie it to a faraway tree. In the meantime, she struggled to widen the bulky sarafan so she could ride comfortably astride.

She kept the horse at a slow pace, taking the time to savor the forest that she might not see again. Early summer blooms and plants had replaced spring wildflowers, and the trees had evolved from lime to a rich malachite green. A doe and two fawns stopped in front of her, and Tatiana reined in the horse to allow them to bound safely away.

Inhaling the sharp scent of pines and the perfumed smell of the season's last wild lilacs, she tried to store up memories for when her life returned to one inside the terem. She savored the sound of crackling branches and last year's decayed leaves beneath the horse's hooves.

A huge fallen oak blocked their path at one point, so she loosened her mount's reins and let him take the lead. Nothing looked as familiar as she had expected, though somehow she believed that Baba's magic, and perhaps a little unseen guidance from the leshi, would bring her to the oak tree residence.

A lapis-colored butterfly had landed on the saddle horn almost as soon as she had left the hut in the clearing, and remained there, as if by magic.

Soon she spotted the giant oak with the chiseled door, and dismounted so she could tie her horse to a thick maple branch just behind the forsythia bush she had hidden behind the first time.

This time she knocked on the door. After only a few moments, Snow opened it and looked at her crossly.

"What do you want, old woman? We don't give handouts to beggars here."

"I have come for two reasons," Tatiana croaked. "First, I must ask if you would like your child returned to you."

Snow started to close the door. Quick as a hare, Tatiana reached out a wizened hand and blocked it half open.

"What child? I have no child." Snow voice's rose an octave.

"Yet you gave birth to one, I presume."

"Presume all you want, you old hag. I am still a young virgin and resent your implications."

So that question was answered. Now Tatiana must try to get her to take the locket.

"Beg your pardon, My Lady. I primarily came here to give you a gift. It is something I found hidden in a special place, and it is much too expensive and delicate for the likes of me."

Curiosity getting the best of her, Snow demanded, "Show me!"

Tatiana opened her gnarled hand and revealed the locket. "It is a golden apple, I believe." She took another chance as she dangled the necklace so that the apple shimmered in the sunshine. "I am told by a witch that it is powerful and valuable and that it belongs to someone of more royal blood than I. She advised me not to use its power, only to give it to a woman much younger."

"Why didn't she keep it herself then?"

"She is a witch. She needs no more power. Or so she explained."

Slowly Snow reached out. Her eyes shone.

Tatiana curled her hands, preventing Snow from taking it yet. "I am willing to give you this priceless, magical locket. Again, though, I must warn you to keep it hidden. Perhaps under your gown. I believe the leshi will covet it and attempt to steal it."

"They *are* a greedy lot. Tell me, what is its power? Might it keep me young forever?"

"This you will learn for yourself. I am sworn to silence. Actually, I know little. Of course, if you do not wish to own it, I will take it to the city. Perhaps to the palace where there are women who might covet it."

"*Nyet*! Give it to me!"

Tatiana opened her hand and Snow snatched the locket.

"You shall wear it then?"

"I suppose I must if it is magic." She slipped it over her head and then, after holding the golden apple out to admire it, tucked the locket under her blouse and out of sight.

"Now be gone!" she commanded as she started to shut the door in Tatiana's face once more.

As she did so, however, Snowdrop dropped to the ground, eyes closed and one hand still placed on her chest where the hidden locket rested.

Unsure what to do, Tatiana attempted to lift Snow and decided to place her on the bed in the tree.

Just then she heard the sound of pounding hooves and voices.

"Ladies! Do you need help?" a familiar voice called out.

"Is the woman ill?" another equally recognizable voice asked as the horsemen reined in.

It was Igor and Mikhail, accompanied by Dimitri.

She gently laid Snow back down and faced them. "It is I—Tanya. I know you don't recognize me. I am under a temporary spell to alter my appearance." She cleared her throat and tried to regain her youthful voice. "You are my father's bogatyrs—sirs Mikhail, Dimitri, and Igor, am I right?" She pointed at each one as she named him.

All three dismounted and ran to her. Igor bent over Snowdrop and checked her pulse.

"We have searched for you for weeks and weeks!" Mikhail cried.

"It seems we have all been ensorcelled ourselves by some kind of spell," Dimitri added. "We are overwhelmed with joy to find you again."

"We thought the worst," Mikhail added.

Igor looked up at them. "This is the Grand Duchess Snowdrop, is it not?"

"It is. She dyed her hair black. Right now she is under a sleeping spell. This is our chance to return her to the Terem Palace."

"What has happened?" Mikhail and Dimitri demanded in chorus.

"I will explain it all on our way back to Moskva. Yet how will we return her?"

"I will set her in front of me on the stallion," Igor volunteered.

"Let's hope she doesn't awaken and try to escape," Tatiana said.

As the four mounted, with Snow carefully held in Igor's arms, Tatiana happened to look behind the hut. The six short leshi did not appear to be at home. She did see the taller one who originally had led her to their forest residence.

He blended in with a copse of maples, glowing faintly blue amidst the leaves. Lifting a branch-like arm covered with acorns, he waved silently. So perhaps the spell had ended, and nothing would interfere with their venture back to the city and the palace.

As she reached for her horse, she waved back. In a flash the forest spirit had vanished.

Chapter 21

Tatiana's hands on the reins grew more youthful and the spots began to fade as the day wore on. When she lifted her hand to her cheeks, they felt softer and smoother than earlier.

They stopped to make camp, with Sir Igor taking over watching Snow. "Why doesn't she wake up? What exactly has happened?"

"I told you, it is a sleeping spell. She will awaken soon—I hope not before we get her back to the palace. I have the distinct impression she does not want to return there."

Convinced Snow slept soundly, Tatiana slowly began to unravel the events of the past few weeks to three men who listened before a blazing fire in a combination of awe and disbelief.

They had no problem believing in Baba Yaga's existence or help, seeming only reassured that all those nights their beloved Tanya had been safe in the infamous hut perched atop the chicken legs. They also had no trouble accepting that the forest spirits had interfered with their own search, which, she noticed, seemed to have left them appearing somewhat haggard. She felt a twinge of guilt.

She still had to lie to them, starting with a complete omission of the part about the baby. It wasn't up to her to reveal that the virgin princess had had an out-of-wedlock child by a poor huntsman or that the grand duchess had given the child away as casually as she tossed aside the peas she disliked on her plate.

"Why did she leave home in the first place?" This question came up several times, however, and Tatiana could only shake her head helplessly.

"I believe she wanted some liberty. And we cannot tell anyone where she was, only that she perhaps fell ill in a peasant's hut and that the woman took care of her." *It would not do*, she thought, *for anyone to suspect she had been free in the forest and prey to anyone, let alone that she had shared quarters with seven men.*

She had mulled all this over on the afternoon's fast-paced ride, and prayed they might get Snow to the palace before she awakened. Tatiana had no wish for Snow to know of her stepmother's involvement, let alone its accompanying witchcraft. No matter what happened when Snow awakened, she must not suspect Tatiana of any knowledge of past events, and Tatiana would beg Alex to keep the secret, as well.

She sighed, realizing that she had become involved in a

tangle of deceits and falsities—and all for the sake of a step-daughter who did not love her.

Just before they reached the city on the following afternoon, they stopped so Tatiana could locate finer clothes from her saddlebags. She was willing to face the scandal of riding into Moskva and up to the palace with the others, despite her cousins all warning against it.

"You must go alone, Your Imperial Highness. We will wait and ride into the Kremlin with Snow much later. That way there will be much less suspicion about your role—and Snow will not know you were with her, let alone that you are aware of her defection and hiding place."

"Yes, of course."

So, riding side saddle in a pearl-encrusted gown and wearing a modest lemon-colored *kokoshnik* similarly covered with pearls, she approached the Kremlin and the Terem Palace.

Cries of joy and amazement arose before she had reached the palace, with people prostrating themselves on the ground as she came in sight.

Before she could get assistance dismounting, Alex had raced out of the palace and swept her into his arms.

"My darling!" he kept repeating, and without asking her any questions, ordered two of his men to spread the word that Tatiana had returned and commanded two others to notify the tsar.

He then swooped her up the palatial stairway to his apartments, where he set her gently on the divan.

As he covered her face and neck and hands with kisses, she barely heard him when he managed to ask, "Where is my daughter?"

"Soon," she assured him. "She will be here soon. Today," she added at his crestfallen look.

Ordering all the curious people out of the room, he then commanded a servant to prepare food and to "bring some French wine to celebrate."

They spent the next few hours talking, with Tatiana choosing some words carefully. It was critical she convince Alex that Snow should not know of her stepmother's involvement. Temporarily ignoring the vow of complete openness and no more secrets that she had made in the forest, she did not mention the pregnancy or the baby yet. There would be plenty of time *if* she chose to enlighten him. Nor did she wish to spoil Snow's homecoming. In the meantime, she *did* tell him about meeting Baba Yaga and receiving the mirror at Tolkov (omitting the later attempted poisoning), fleeing via the secret passageway in his room, staying with the witch in the forest, discovering Snow hiding with the forest spirits, and tricking her into falling asleep via a spell.

"I'm convinced she was not held against her will," she told him. "I believe that after being secluded for her entire life in a palace terem, she thought she needed some freedom. The leshi were kind enough to take her in when they found her in the forest, and I can assure you that she was not harmed."

"Perhaps you are correct about her yearning for freedom. She has always been headstrong and unhappy—even before her mother died."

"That was a tragedy that also may have taken its toll," Tatiana murmured, then, remembering Baba's suspicions, she shivered beside the flaming hearth.

"Tanya, there is something you must know. I feel awful

speaking ill of the dead, but unfortunately my marriage was a disaster. It was a marriage of convenience, yes, but I don't believe that either of us ever really cared for one another. All our joint appearances as a loving couple were a façade." Then, taking both her hands in his, he added earnestly, "You are the first and only woman I have ever loved. I hope you can believe that."

Tears of joy ran down Tatiana's cheeks. "I do believe you, Alex. And you must know that I love you, too." Before she could continue, he was kissing her eyelids and covering her face and neck with more kisses.

When he finally stopped, he pulled back and looked into her eyes. "I do know from the few ambassadors who travel to Moskva and Yaroslavl that women in other kingdoms are not imprisoned—as it must surely seem to some of them—in their palaces. Certainly women not of the nobility have plenty of freedom here. It appears that changes need to be made in this tsardom, as well."

"I love you," she told her husband once more. "You have no idea how much."

"And I love you! I've been out of my mind with grief, and if you hadn't left me two letters or notes, I fear I might have jumped from the tallest belfry to my death. Seriously," he said intently, wrapping her in his arms even though she still balanced a wine glass in one hand.

Tatiana reached in her pouch and unwrapped both Baba's blessing and the snowflake obsidian locket. "I shall come to no harm with this locket," she assured him, explaining its powers. She did not add that it was harm from his daughter that she feared.

Now he insisted on presenting her to his father. They did require a believable story—and one that would not offend the church's priests and clergy. They decided to tell the tsar that Tatiana had received a message swearing her to secrecy and advising her where to find Snow. She would explain she had spent these past weeks helping a peasant woman take care of Snow and was unable to get a message back home. It was a flimsy story. However, they prayed the tsar would not only find it credible, yet would go along with the added deception about Tatiana's purported lack of involvement.

Fortunately, the tsar asked few questions. The experience of having both a granddaughter and a daughter-in-law missing for most of the spring and summer had taken its toll, and he was only too relieved at having the latter back home and the promise that the former would arrive soon.

In the meantime, bells reverberated across the city and through the Kremlin. They rang more profusely (so that most residents had to cover their ears) right before the evening meal when a knight arrived bearing Snow's sleeping form.

Apparently Sir Igor had made an agreement with the others to show up alone, lest there be a means of ferreting the truth out of three more easily than one. He ordered some of the tsar's men to carry Snow up to her terem and called for the imperial physicians to meet them there. In the confusion over whether this black-haired beauty in a simple gown was in fact their beloved golden-haired princess, Igor managed to slip away.

The chaos continued as imperial physicians, healers, and sorcerers consulted and argued regarding Snowdrop's condition.

Two days later, Tatiana was able to spend time alone with Olga and Sonya, both overjoyed at her return. With them she spared no details, and it felt liberating to be able to tell them about Snowdrop's baby as well as all the other unusual things that had befallen her.

"Sir Mikhail sent a message," Olga told her. "All three of your father's cousins have headed to Tolkov to give your father the news—not to mention to avoid questioning by anyone who suspects their involvement. They are certain that Sir Nicholas will want to come to Moskva himself to feel assured of your safety and good health."

"I cannot wait to see him!"

Within days, the kingdom began to settle down again, though rumors of all sorts continued to fly. Suggestions of illicit magic also made the rounds, especially after it became apparent that all the healers had failed, and Grand Duchess Snowdrop would not or could not awaken.

***

A week passed before Alex had Snow moved to a special smaller throne room where they could check on her regularly. The tsar ordered an extraordinary crystal bed that revealed her sleeping form while she rested on a thick mattress with gold-threaded pillows and blankets. To Tatiana it resembled a bier supporting a coffin.

Everyone had continued to attempt to feed her or coax liquids down Snow's throat. Nothing worked. Inexplicably, however, Snowdrop remained very much alive, breathing regularly and occasionally emitting a small sigh as if dreaming.

Soon word of the beautiful sleeping princess encased above a crystal platform spread through the land, and people lined up outside the Kremlin palaces to pray and to plead to see her.

The tsar and Alex would have none of it. They continued to summon physicians, healers, clergy, and eventually known sorcerers to try to awaken Snow. Yet no cures, chants, potions, or spells made one iota of difference.

Alex demanded that another piece of crystal be perched atop the bier-like bed to protect his daughter's head from well-wishers and those who fruitlessly sought a remedy.

Tatiana watched and worried along with Alex. Both knew this was Baba Yaga's spell, but dared share with no one such controversial information. Tatiana did pull out the magic mirror daily. It stubbornly revealed nothing. She knew Baba had promised her the grand duchess would come to no harm, though surely the magic of the golden locket should have worn off long ago. Was this Baba's way of punishing Snow for her evilness? Should she try to sneak into the little throne room and remove the locket? Would it make any difference?

It was easier not to think or worry about Snow when Lord Nicholas arrived. Ecstatically happy to see her father after so long, she spent several days and part of the evenings in his company.

The warm and respectful relationship between him and the grand duke served as a special delight. Late into the night in the imperial apartments, Alex and her father talked, sipped vodka, and played chess. Often Tatiana sat on the satin armchair and just listened and watched.

"I realize you never will have time to assume the rule of Tolkov, my dear," her father said. "So I leave it to you whom to name as heir."

"Thank you, Father. I will attempt to choose wisely. Unless you have a particular lady in mind who might precede me in the succession?"

He laughed and dismissed her suggestion. "After being married to your mother, I shall never love again," he added, attempting to sound light-hearted.

On her father's last night in Moskva, the court played host to a French storyteller. He had often related a story heard in France about a gorgeous princess who had fallen asleep for one hundred years due to an evil fairy's spell: only a handsome prince's kiss could revive her. The tale spread, and now people began to fear their own princess might be asleep longer than any of them would live.

That night a storyteller related the same legend to the accompaniment of a gusli player picking at his instrument's strings. The tsar, likewise, was picking at course number seventeen: grouse with creamed lemon sauce. As he listened, however, he put down his eating utensils and suddenly pushed away from the table and stood.

"This is what I command!" he said loudly. The music stopped, and everyone, including the grand duke and duchess, paused with forks halfway to their mouths.

"Henceforth I invite every Russian man of noble birth to present himself at the throne room where our grand duchess sleeps. If any of them can awaken her with a word or a touch, he shall share in my wealth and that of her father. Princess

Snowdrop shall then be given in marriage to the noble gentleman."

The tsar's secretary scrambled to write all this down, having learned to travel nowhere in the Kremlin without parchment and quill. He then scurried to his office to ensure that an official notice be copied by all the scribes for distribution throughout the tsardom.

Chapter 22

They streamed into the city from all over Rus, regardless of how many weeks it had taken for the message to reach them or how many versts they had to travel from faraway corners of the realm.

Some of the potential suitors were unmarried, others widowed. Still others had put aside their wives by locking them in convents. All, however, had some claim to nobility. Thus for weeks and then months, princes, counts, dukes, barons, lords, and titled knights arrived to await their turn to see and potentially awaken the sleeping princess. They came from all the greatest and smallest families: the Kurbsys, Obolenskys, Stroganovs, Shuiskys, Polovnas, Sorskys . . .

The men's elaborate kaftans with floor-length sleeves braided in gold and adorned with matching gold and diamond buttons competed in a rainbow of violets, oranges, reds, purples, greens, blues, and yellows. To Tatiana it appeared as if an array of tropical birds flitted in and out, turning the throne room into a tropical aviary.

The patriarch himself, accompanied by four archbishops and an endless parade of black-robed priests, arrived weekly to bless the sleeping figure and to utter Old Church Slavonic chants. Priests dutifully shook elaborately designed silver incense censors, emitting a heavy sweet scent that nearly overwhelmed that of the host of candles burning around the platformed bed. To Tatiana the room seemed stiflingly hot.

Hundreds of icons also had been brought in and attached to the walls. Potential suitors kissed a few in the traditional manner before approaching Snowdrop. They then put their lips to the crystal, seeming to float above her face. Some touched and held her folded hands.

Regardless of what each man said or did, nothing changed. Atop what Tatiana now considered a pedestal, Snow slept obliviously.

"I don't know what else to do," Alex moaned on one of their regular visits to the Princess or Tsarevna Room, as it was now called.

Tatiana stared down at the sleeping girl sadly. Somehow this must be her own fault. Baba had not advised her to remove Snow's locket, and now she saw no way of reaching it without causing an outcry by the dozens of onlookers who perpetually milled around.

"She will awaken, my dear. I just don't know when." She had told Alex about the golden apple and her knowledge that

Snow still wore it, but he was afraid to violate her sanctity by attempting to remove the locket himself.

"I believe if we can just loosen it so it dangles outside her clothing the spell might lift," Tatiana offered, "although I will try to detach it completely."

That same evening, hours past dinner and after the long line of suitors and priests had dwindled, they decided to make an attempt.

"I would like to be alone with my daughter," Alex told the guards. "Please clear the room so that the grand duchess and I may pray."

"Not so difficult after all," Tatiana whispered.

Standing right where the overhead crystal stopped and Snow's body—now in a silver brocade gown—was uncovered below the waist, Tatiana bent down. She deftly reached up for the back of Snow's head. Lifting the girl's lustrous hair, she managed to extract the chain. Alas, she could not loosen it enough to get it over her head.

"His Imperial Majesty!" a guard called out, announcing the arrival of the tsar.

Hastily Tatiana arranged the locket over the gown so that the golden apple was visible.

"What is this?" the tsar, striding up behind them, demanded. Tatiana had straightened, and seconds later the tsar now clearly could see the locket arranged below her neckline.

"It is a special charm, Father. We believe it can awaken her. It has been blessed by Saint Basil," Alex added hastily when the tsar frowned.

"Very well. We have tried everything else to wake my

granddaughter." Now his shoulders, already weighed down by heavy golden robes, sagged. "I am beside myself."

"As are we all, Your Imperial Majesty," Tatiana murmured. "Her father and I pray hourly for her, and with so many prayers uttered and candles lit by your subjects throughout the kingdom, surely things will change soon."

He sighed heavily. "Not if there is magic involved. That old woman with whom she stayed must have put a spell on her. Based on your description, I've sent an army of searchers out to find her hut."

"And no luck, Father?" Alex asked nervously.

The tsar's crown nearly slipped off as he shook his head sadly.

Tatiana knew the phony description would yield nothing. And as for Baba Yaga herself, the witch would not be found if she did not choose to be, and chances were that she had long since left this particular forest for another. The searchers would discover nothing.

***

Autumn arrived in all its bejeweled glory, and Tatiana could not get enough of carriage rides. Encouraged by her husband, she also walked the gardens regularly with Sonya and Olga, and once Alex took her for a stroll just into the edge of the forest. Surrounded as they were by guards, it was difficult to spot any birds or wildlife. Still, she appreciated the gesture and delighted in the array of glistening, patterned ruby, citrine, and topaz leaves dancing their way to the forest floor.

"We must get you more air," he said. " You are free to

spend all the time you want in your own terem or outside, though admittedly I desire to have you in my apartments at night."

Tatiana blushed, recalling countless intimate encounters of late. "Of course, I will come to your bed each night if you so wish it."

"*That* is, of course, one thing I desire. However, it no longer makes any sense to me for a wife—even a royal one—to live separate from her husband. Henceforth the terem rooms may function as your study or sewing area. You belong with me the rest of the time. Does that meet with your approval, dearest?"

It did. Admittedly, they already had spent days and now weeks in his apartments since she returned home. She had thought he might suggest she return to her own bedchamber any day, and the idea of not having to do so delighted her.

Eventually their visits to Snow dwindled in frequency, and Tatiana guiltily had to admit to herself that she enjoyed a sense of relaxation hitherto unenjoyed in the Kremlin. She felt safe from attempted poisonings and released from having her stepdaughter scowl at her.

She did not forget her responsibility to the princess, however. "Should we have her bathed and her clothing changed?" she asked Countess Tsergaya and Alex.

"Surprisingly, it does not seem necessary," Alex replied.

"She smells fresh, like lemons and almonds," the countess reminded her.

And so, undisturbed, Snowdrop slept. And slept.

***

With the snow-coated trees now denuded of leaves and travel more challenging during the early winter, fewer and fewer travelers visited the gilded Princess Room. Only groups of church women hovered inside, industriously polishing icons, dusting the crystal bed, or endlessly tending and replacing the hundreds of candles.

As for the apple locket, much of the attention it had garnered at first died down. "It is a charm to protect her while she sleeps," Tatiana overheard one woman mention to another.

"Surely she is protected from evil this way. And her new black hair provides a disguise to keep evil spirits away."

Such comments gradually had evolved into a popular theory for the large contingent of believers in magic and sorcery.

However, another day she heard two nuns discussing the interminable sleep just outside the church. "That locket is a holy symbol of Eve's forbidden apple."

"She must have sinned grievously," the other responded.

"Heresy. Certainly God's punishment."

This particular conversation made Tatiana a little nervous, and she worried people would suspect something untoward had occurred while the princess was absent for so long.

Fortunately, a third group of priests, holy fools, and devoted Christians venerated the tsarevna. With her white as snow skin, long lashes gracing her cheeks, and silken black hair fanned out on the pillow, she did look almost virginal.

This last theory tempted Tatiana to laugh, and inevitably she had to draw her veil closer around her face and mouth.

***

One afternoon when few bystanders occupied the room, an unusually reclusive count from Novgorod arrived to be one of the last to attempt the awakening. His knee-high white boots dripped melted snow on the marble floor.

Just as he bent to kiss the crystal covering, he slipped on the water and crashed into the crystal case!

Everyone, including Alex and Tatiana, gasped. They ran to the princess as the bier wobbled, thankfully without collapsing or splintering.

Relieved, everyone started to relax until suddenly the count shouted, "She's awake!"

Tatiana and Alex, still nearby, stared at Snow's face. Indeed, her eyes were wide open.

"The locket! Look!" Tatiana whispered urgently to Alex, who had rushed off to order a group of servants wiping down the room to find assistance.

Indeed, something unusual had happened. The golden apple, which Tatiana had assumed was solid, had split open, revealing a pearlescent lining. Cradled inside she could just make out something tiny and honey-hued. A piece of amber perhaps?

There was no time to ponder this, let alone reach for the locket, as Snow's eyes moved frantically around before locking on the handsome count's face.

"Can you speak, my dear daughter?" Alex demanded. "No, don't try to get up," he added, as she struggled to do so without speaking.

By this time he'd found servants to help himself and the count lift the crystal cover off his daughter.

Snowdrop sat up, yawning. "Why is everyone here? And where are we, father?"

"It is a long story. You are safe," he repeated twice while helping her to her feet.

The count who had bumped into the crystal coffin asked permission before swooping the princess into his arms and following Alex out the door. Tatiana hurriedly followed.

"I do not understand why I am in public—and without my ladies," Snow protested to her father. "And how did I come to be here?"

Taking advantage of the distraction, Tatiana rapidly reached up behind them and yanked the locket off Snow's neck.

"It is almost a fairytale, my princess," the count replied. "And perhaps the happiest day of my life."

Before they could reach a less public place, the first chimes of what would become a bell crescendo began.

Chapter 23

His name was Count Lekov, and he had lost his first wife to smallpox. Many nobles joked that she just as well could have died of boredom. This supposition came from the count's habit of taking frequent leave of his palace outside Novgorod for up to two years at a time. He devoted every hour to conquering faraway lands and establishing concurrent castles and villages. While this made him an asset to his lord the tsar, it meant he devoted scant time to court festivities, let alone his late wife and three rambunctious boys.

Snowdrop, whether or not she had qualms about this ready-made family, may have looked forward to having a husband who would abandon her for long stretches of time. Tatiana surmised that there was, after all, no reason to believe Snow felt anything more than relief at getting married and escaping any potential scandal—let alone accusations of treason.

Now that Snow had awakened, Tatiana decided she should begin to wear the snowflake obsidian necklace from Baba Yaga. Even busily engaged with wedding preparations, her stepdaughter could not have turned suddenly trustworthy.

Sitting in her bedchamber after her breakfast tray had been removed a couple days later, Tatiana also decided on a whim to pull out the mirror. Perhaps she should not have been surprised when once again it chanted in a musical voice:

> *The day she will be the most fair*
> *Is the day you must beware.*
> *No matter the gift of something rare*
> *Do not agree to wear the pear.*

This made absolutely no sense. When she repeated the looking glass's warning to Olga and Sonya, they were equally mystified.

"You do eat a lot of pears," Sonya observed. "Though why would you 'wear' one?"

"Perhaps the mirror refers to a piece of jewelry," Olga suggested. "Someone—probably the grand duchess—might attempt to give you a golden pear just like her golden apple from Baba Yaga."

"Perhaps," Tatiana mused. "And I am certain the chant refers to Snow's wedding day, when she assuredly will be 'most fair.'"

She could do little more than resolve to "beware" of the girl until she had left the Kremlin once and for all.

Sensing a lack of enthusiasm by his daughter at becoming a bride, Alex commented to Snowdrop frequently on the solitudinous count's handsome visage, sandy blonde hair, neat matching beard, and meticulous clothing.

"And Count Lekov is quite intellectual," he added while having tea with his wife and daughter one afternoon before the wedding.

"What does that mean?" Snow asked.

"Just that he enjoys books and studies, as well as atlases and map-making. I'm certain he could teach you much about the world."

Tatiana almost choked on her piece of biscuit and gooseberry jam.

"I know more than you suspect, my dear father," Snow said confidently.

"That is fine to hear, if you presumably mean about astronomy, alchemy, the history of our tsardom, and maps of the world," he said wryly.

"I know enough, I suppose."

Alex frowned at his daughter, and again Tatiana tried not to laugh as this time she envisioned the count reading aloud by the fireside to his infinitely bored young wife.

"Your stepmother is a scholar as well, of course," Alex added proudly.

When Snow merely rolled her eyes and departed, though, he sighed. "I don't know exactly where I went wrong with my daughter. She had the finest tutors and clergymen in the land to instruct her, yet I sense there is somewhat not quite right about her. Not to mention I suspect a bit of a void occupies that beautiful head."

"Don't forget that she managed to escape the Kremlin and stay hidden throughout an entire summer. That took cunning and planning."

"Oh, I do not forget. In fact, her new maids and ladies report directly to Countess Tsargaya now. There shall be no more dangerous pranks until she is at least safely in Novgorod. Perhaps this is unneeded, since she claims no memory of recent events."

Snow and Count Lekov—whose "rescue" of her and thus his accidental bridal *prize* were accepted by everyone—were to marry only days later. That meant wedding preparations took up everyone's time, attention, and energy; any more gossip about the princess's mysterious vanishment and enchanted sleep had earned less attention than it might have.

Although purporting to recall nothing about her experiences during her disappearance, Snowdrop provided Tatiana one clue that this was not true: the princess developed a habit of absentmindedly grasping the area at her neckline where the golden apple locket had resided for so long.

Since Snowdrop begrudgingly deferred only to Countess Tsargaya and made it clear she needed no planning assistance from her stepmother, Tatiana divided her own time between her husband and her ladies.

The latter expressed excitement about the festivities, and one of the best seamstresses immediately set to work creating a crimson sarafan lavishly embroidered with roses of gold thread. The woman also, at Tatiana's request, embroidered green-leafed rosebuds down the billowing sleeves A towering red *kokoshnik* bedecked with rubies and garnets scattered down to her hair, and her forehead would be elegantly draped with gold veils made from fine Belgian lace. Alex had lavished her with rings and bracelets to match, until the only item missing was a pair of slippers.

The shoes arrived in a silver box, which Olga brought in only hours before the festivities. "These were just delivered," she said. "I'm not certain who ordered them." She gasped with awe as she removed them from their case.

"Let me wear my own wedding slippers for the ceremony and banquet; just bring these along for the ballroom dancing," Tatiana decided after seeing the delicate beauty of the host of diamonds and rubies loosely attached to the red brocade slippers.

The wedding took place in the slightly smaller though equally elaborate Annunciation Cathedral. It was Tatiana's favorite, with its nine sparkling gold domes, four of which resembled golden helmets. Since it connected directly to Terem Palace, initially the tsar and then the bride entered at the front and Tatiana could only see Snowdrop's royal purple dress and lavender veils. Her hair had once again grown at least halfway back to its original pale color, falling in two half-blond braids down her back.

The ceremony ran much shorter than Tatiana's and Alex's, yet seemed to last forever. At least Tatiana was allowed to stand beside her beloved husband rather than behind a screen, as she did for most sermons and services. She steadfastly avoided watching the bride, while eyeing the handsome, joyful groom with pity.

Meanwhile she savored the cathedral's murals of biblical and historical figures, the altar's agate and jasper floor, and the multiple antechambers and frescoed alcoves now crowded with guests. Behind the sumptuous iconostasis, she knew, was the private entrance leading to the tsar's chambers.

The seventy-dish feast also seemed to drag. Tatiana looked forward to the dancing that would come next.

"Where are the diamond-coated red slippers?" Tatiana asked when Alex began to walk from table to table greeting the boyars and other noble guests.

In due time Olga arrived with the silver box and then seated herself in Alex's empty chair to help.

"What a stunning pair!" Sonya remarked as Tatiana edged out of her original gold slippers to trade them before the opening dance.

Just as Tatiana started to slide her tiny left foot into the red slipper, three things occurred rapidly and almost simultaneously.

Her left toes where the slipper touched them grew warm, then hot. In seconds she perceived a pain as intense as if she had dipped her toes in flames.

Before she could pull off the slipper, Olga gasped: "It's a *pair* of shoes—not *pear* the fruit. 'Do not agree to wear the *pair*.' Help!"

Tatiana yanked at her neck and swiftly pulled out the obsidian locket. She dangled it over her now bare and scalding toes, and then swung the stone across both red slippers. Each began to emit smoke.

"What is happening?" Alex cried, seeing all the terrified faces and the smoking shoes as he approached. He looked at the snowflake obsidian locket in his wife's hand and his face tightened.

"It's Snow again!" Olga cried. "Once more she has atte-mpted to murder My Lady—Her Imperial Highness."

"Snow? Murder? What do you mean 'once more?'"

Sweeping his wife into his arms, he hurried them out of the ballroom and into an antechamber, Olga and Sonya at his heels.

Aware of a trailing audience and his wife's pain, Alex rushed them all into the square where they would not be overheard and he could dip his wife's feet into a gurgling fountain of cold water.

It took a long time to get to the truth, or at least the parts Tatiana, Olga, and Sonya were willing to share. In the end, the fact that pierced through what might have been Alex's previous sense of denial was that his daughter was infinitely wicked—and affiliated with malevolent magic.

"Your Imperial Highness," Sir Oleg came up behind them. "All of the guests and His Majesty himself await your wed-ding toast."

"Let them wait."

"Sir Oleg," Tatiana said breathlessly. "It is critical that I speak with Her Highness the tsarevna. In my husband's quarters. Alone!"

Open-mouthed, Sir Oleg did not glance at his lord for per-mission. "Right away, Your Imperial Highness."

"Are you certain?" Alex asked Tatiana, his face beginning to twist in something between grief and anger.

She was. Placing her original wedding slippers back on her feet, she strode back inside the Terem Palace where the feast was being held.

"Follow me in ten minutes," she called to Alex and her ladies.

Regardless of her surprise at being hauled out of her own wedding banquet by Sir Oleg, Snowdrop showed up almost immediately, looking guilty. And sullen. She must have witnessed or heard something about the scene in the banquet hall.

Tatiana faced her angrily, clenching her fists at her sides. One of them still grasped the black obsidian locket. Just in case. Her voice hardened as she ordered the Grand Duchess—now Countess Lekov—to remain standing.

"Let me explain this to you once, and only once. I know many things about you that I am certain you do not wish exposed."

Snow tossed her almost golden braids and for a moment dropped the mask of civility that she had worn throughout the wedding. "I doubt that."

"Never doubt that. I know, for example, that you are no virgin."

Snow put up her hand, the emerald wedding ring flashing beneath the candlelit chandelier. "Nonsense."

"I know," Tatiana continued harshly, "that you allowed yourself to be bedded by a commoner—a huntsman—and that you gave birth to his child."

Snow's mouth snapped shut.

"I also know that you abandoned the child as if it were leftovers from dinner, not to mention that you lived with seven men."

"Not *men*," Snow muttered.

Now it was Tatiana's turn to put up her hand. "Enough!

Know this: should you ever again make an attempt on my life or that of your father or that of any of our future children, all shall be revealed. There are now many others who know everything about you if something should befall me. I assure you that if the truth about you becomes known, you shall spend the rest of your life locked in a convent. Or perhaps burned at the stake."

Gasping, Snow stood back and gazed at her stepmother with hate-filled eyes.

"Go to your new husband tonight," Tatiana ordered. "Convince him you have never been with a man. Then retreat to your fine new residence and remain there. I do not wish to see you at court in the future. Do you understand?"

Snow nodded, remaining silent.

As she whirled around to leave, Tatiana added, "And absolutely no harm should come to your groom! We will expect the Count Lekov to remain *healthy*, as well."

Snowdrop's eyes burned with blue fire. She lifted her dress as if prepared to storm back to her wedding feast.

Only then did Tatiana, as she sensed her husband entering the room, realize that she had been trembling during the entire confrontation. Alex placed an arm around her and glared at his daughter.

Once again she recalled Baba's words about secrets, and grasped anew that some must be kept to protect the ones you love. She would never bring such grief to Alex, and felt relieved he had not entered the room in time to hear the entire conversation.

Nevertheless, a furious prince confronted his daughter.

"What you have done is evil! I shall not permit you ever again to harm my wife—or anyone else."

"Father, I had no idea! I don't know anything about magic. And I've never seen those shoes before!"

"You've always lied, Snowdrop. I know nothing of you anymore, certainly not who you are or why you have turned against your own stepmother. And I strongly suspect—in fact I know—that this is not the first time you have used magic to endanger someone!"

Snow shook her head emphatically as her father and stepmother walked out, leaving her to make her own way to the banquet hall.

Tatiana knew in her heart that Snow would vanish from her life for good. Comprehending that her stepmother knew so much about her and was willing to publicize the truth would be enough to dissuade her from any further acts of evil.

An hour later, just before the five dessert courses were born into the room, Alexander followed the tsar's toast and gifts with one of his own.

"My wedding gift to Count Lokov of Novgorod," he announced loudly, "is a large parcel of tillable land in the vast unsettled territory of Siber. My wife, the Imperial Highness Tatiana, graciously has agreed to grant you a large palace along the Siberian River Ob, as well. We realize that this means we shall see little of the newlyweds when they and all their children are settled a journey of many months away— and with so much responsibility. We will look forward to them sending messages to us when the mountain passes clear."

Murmurs of surprise and approval filled the room, where

the royal guests waited to attack the first of their delicate desserts. Everyone knew that the frozen Siber, with its incredible distance well beyond the Ural Mountains, its vast taiga, its bitterly cold climate, its ever-present snow, and its life of hardships, required more than miners and prisoners in exile. It needed management and colonization. How kind of Grand Duke Alexander and Grand Duchess Tatiana to grace their daughter and her groom with such an honor, especially knowing the count's fascination with settling new lands.

Tatiana glanced at Snowdrop, whose face had turned as white as her name. She then smiled graciously at their guests, knowing in all likelihood this would be the last time she would ever see her evil stepdaughter.

Epilogue

A year passed. And then another. The tsar seemed to regain his health and strength, perhaps in part due to the herbal remedy Tatiana had concocted. Combined with her own knowledge and what she had learned from Baba Yaga, she had convinced the imperial healers to consult with her. The resulting treatment appeared to work well enough to ensure the tsar's continued health.

This pleased Tatiana for many reasons. Both she and Alex were willing to work diligently on royal business, yet neither was in a hurry to inherit the throne.

She would always long for adventure and the outdoors, although more and more Tatiana grew to appreciate spending time in the royal gardens, now expanded under her direction.

Especially during the winter, she strolled the gardens with her twin sons—the new grand dukes. Together they delighted in the enchanted fairyland where a blade of grass presented itself as a jeweled wonder. When the sun broke through heavy pewter clouds, every bush and tree sparkled and preened, as if a grateful God had dropped buckets of diamonds upon the gardens.

Three years after liberating Snow from her crystal bubble, Count Lokov presented himself to his tsar and his tsarevich in Moskva.

"It has been an amazing experience living in Siber," he noted, and then proceeded to make an enthusiastic report to his sovereigns about the mining and timber interests he had established.

The news from his fortification along the massive River Ob was also joyful: Countess Snowdrop had given birth to twin girls, now two years old.

Tatiana smiled rather smugly. She thought of her own twins safe in the terem with their nurses, servants, and Sonya—now the royal tutor. "How long is the journey, Count?"

"More than six months. Much less without my wife slowing us down as she did after our wedding. The countess—I mean the grand duchess—will never be able to tolerate such suffering again. In fact, she complains bitterly about the difficulties of the trip to this day." He smiled indulgently before continuing.

"Even if she could bear the rugged travel, she would not have been able to do so," he added, then announced proudly that Snowdrop had been with child when he departed. "No doubt the child will be nearly a year old before I return." Since Snow, who had not wanted her one baby, had married a man with three children, this meant she would be burdened with six to raise and control. Tatiana could not help smile at the poetic justice of it all.

That evening she consulted the mirror. As usual, it only gleamed back at her. All continued to be well.

At dinner her father, Lord Nicholas, sat across from the count and next to his daughter.

Since Lord Tolkov also traveled frequently, and often the same vast distances as the count, the two shared tales of their encounters with wolves, bears, and native peoples.

"So many adventures and obstacles," the count observed. "I think my oddest experience was the first trip to Siberia with my wife Snowdrop. For some reason we were traveling in a circle for the entire third month. No matter which way our party went, we ended up back in the same part of the forest. We never moved a verst. Strange."

Tatiana smiled to herself. So perhaps the leshi had gotten their revenge by having some fun with Snowdrop at her husband's expense. She could imagine the spoiled young duchess forced to endure an extra miserable month sleeping on the ground and shivering day and night as they struggled to maneuver carts, horses, and livestock through the forests and the neck-high snow.

"You arrived too late for a wedding, Count," Lord Nicholas interrupted her thoughts. "My bogatyr, Sir Dimitri, was wed recently to my daughter's chief lady in waiting, Olga Vasilievna."

"Ah, I remember Sir Dimitri well," the count said. "And Olga, of course. I would have liked to attend. Perhaps we can spend some time together while I am here."

"I'm afraid that will not be possible on this visit," Tatiana said. "He and Olga have returned to Tolkov for the summer."

"Sir Dimitri is preparing to assume the lordship of my principality," Lord Nicholas added. "Thanks to my daughter, who has graciously turned over her title to Olga."

There was more wonderful news, of course, but Tatiana found herself drifting off. Rarely did she miss the independence to explore the forest anymore. She loved having her father in Moskva so frequently. Occasionally he took her out to hunt or just explore the edge of the forest to gather herbs (accompanied, of course, by a dozen of Alex's men). When the weather was less cooperative, he rode with her carriage through the square where St. Basil's architectural medley still overwhelmed her as much as it had on the day she and Masha had first seen it on their secret visit.

It had been on one such carriage outing to the square with just Sonya that Tatiana accidentally had located Kristina, the woman who had taken in Snowdrop's baby. She and her husband worked as saddle makers in a small shop on the square's edge.

"I must stop here," she had ordered the driver. She beckoned the woman she had recognized to approach the carriage.

"How is your child?" she asked.

Kristina did not recognize Tatiana as the huntsman and then the old lady who had appeared in Baba Yaga's hut. She pointed to her husband and an adorable little girl with hair spun like gold. The two were enthralled by a nearby puppeteer.

"She is wonderful, my Olga. The light of her father's life. And of mine."

Knowing that the family had no idea Grand Duchess Snowdrop had given birth to the girl, Tatiana merely handed her a small bag containing several gold coins. "For the little girl," she said simply.

A puzzled albeit grateful Kristina accepted the money. "Your Imperial Highness is generous. God has been good to us." She curtsied, then bowed, unsure of the proper protocol for accepting a gift from this amazing tsarevna who for some reason had given her actual gold.

After that, Tatiana would ask a servant or Sonya to drop into the small shop with extra food and sometimes coins. At her encouragement, all of Alex's knights began to order their equine gear from that particular business. She felt no guilt at the deception, as the child seemed to be thriving in her permanent home. She also considered anyone who escaped life with Snowdrop for her mother to be fortunate indeed.

Seeing Kristina made her think about Baba Yaga, and Tatiana wondered if she might encounter her again. Occasionally she took out the matryoshka doll that Baba had given her and thought back to her visits and then her stay with the wise crone who'd done so much for her.

Sometimes at night she tossed and turned, pondering whether Baba Yaga's suspicions about Princess Natalya being poisoned by her own daughter could be true. If so, should she continue to harbor such an awful secret? Eventually she accepted that some secrets should be kept, at least until a more appropriate time. Whether such an occasion would ever arise, she did not know. For now she did not need to decide.

She loved her husband with all her heart. With Snow out of their lives, Tatiana still had plenty of time to make difficult decisions. In the meantime, she cuddled against Alex's sleeping body in the imperial bed with the velvet curtains.

After all, morning was always wiser than the evening.

Author's Note

This novel corresponds most closely to the Grimms' version of "Snow White and the Seven Dwarfs," which contains elements that Disney viewers, for example, might not recognize. In the Grimms' edition, the stepmother makes three attempts to poison Snow White: once with a comb, once with lace, and once with the apple. The ending features the stepmother being forced to dance to her death in red hot shoes. (See the URL below for an online version.)

Inspiration for the novel came from one of my own poems, "That Queen," which retells the tale from the stepmother's point of view and appears in my award-winning chapbook, *Rapunzel's Hair* (All Nations Press). The setting came to me naturally based on my background as a specialist in Russian culture, not to mention approximately thirty trips to that country. The final piece of inspiration fell into place after I saw two oil paintings by Russian artist Konstantin Mayovsky (1839-1915): *The Bride Show* (in Moscow's Tretyakov Gallery; see next pg.) and *A Boyar Wedding Feast* (at Hillwood Estate in Washington, DC).

All characters in the novel are fictional (with the exception of previous bride show contestants who really were destroyed or even murdered by their competitors), meaning you won't find this particular tsar and tsarevich in the history books. However, all settings—with the exception of Tolkov—are based on actual places: Moscow, Yaroslavl, Siber(ia), the River Ob, and all of the referenced cathedrals and palaces. Other details were intended to fit roughly into the late seventeenth century, after the awful period known as the Time of Troubles and just prior to Peter the Great's reign. Hence specifics regarding royal protocol, costumes, the treatment of women, tunnels, knights, etc. belong in that era. Any errors are mine, although I did take some literary license due to the folktale genre.

Baba Yaga and the leshi play important roles in Slavic myth and folklore. Baba Yaga, in particular, is presented in many guises and has inspired multiple interpretations over the centuries. Due to the Orthodox Church's prohibitions, no Russian folktales were published in that country until ethnographer Alexander Afanas'ev released the first part of his comprehensive collection in 1855. Until that time, folktales were passed down strictly via oral tradition.

To read the 7th edition (1857) of the Grimm Brothers' version, the best and easiest place to go is to this link: https://sites.pitt.edu/~dash/grimm053.html

Devushka in a Kokhosnik
Artist: Konstantin Makovsky

Paintings and drawings depicting kokoshniks (headdresses), kaftans, sarafans, and the medieval Russian bridal contest. To see them in color, visit www.rypmabooks.com or take a look at the colorized photos of ball costumes worn by Nicholas II and Alexandra plus their guests to celebrate 290 years of Romanov rule. The best of these can be found on Russia Beyond's website: https://www.rbth.com/history/335929-last-ball-romanov

Photograph of Countess Olga Orlova
in early 17th-century costume

An imperial kaftan

1903 Romanov medieval costume ball

The Choice of the Bride Artist: Grigory Sedov
(portrayal of Tsar Alexis I at bride show in 1648)

Men's clothing and kaftans from Old Russia.
Drawing by Adolf Rosenberg

Suggested Book Club Discussion Questions

1. Did you find Lady Tanya's reactions to her predicament when called to the Bride Show believable? What about when she "wins" the contest? If not, what else would you have expected from her?
2. In what ways does the forest setting(s) drive the plot, besides the obvious? Does it also enhance or reflect the narrative or the characters symbolically? Examples?
3. What are some "forbidden" places, situations, objects, and even people that Tanya finds a way to defy?
4. What are some key symbols in the novel and how do they enhance the narrative? One example might be the looking glass/mirror. Another might be the nested doll, as one critic points out.
5. Besides her defiance, in what ways is Tatiana a strong and brave woman—or when is she not? What about Snowdrop?

6. Does this novel feel at all feminist? What aspects of gender discrimination so prevalent back then still affect contemporary society?

7. If you were at all familiar with Baba Yaga beforehand, in what ways does she fit other depictions and in what ways does she add new dimensions to the mythological character?

8. Do the descriptions of the medieval and imperial Russian setting engage your interest—or distract from the plot? Can you find favorite or least favorite portions?

9. Can you find instances of foreshadowing (seemingly insignificant hints or clues of later events) in the first several chapters?

10. If you've read the Grimm Brothers' "Snow White and the Seven Dwarfs," how does the narrator find creative ways to incorporate certain elements of that tale into this novel? Think, for example, about the 3 attempts to "kill" Snow White (comb, lace, apple) and the fate of the stepmother.

11. Besides the characters of Baba Yaga and the Leshi, did you notice references to other mythology/folktales/legends? If so, where?

12. Did you find the sex and/or love scenes between Alexander and Tatiana believable or well handled?

13. In what ways did you find the Epilogue satisfying (or not)?

14. Have you read any other novelized retellings of folktales intended for an adult audience? If so, how does this compare to some of your favorites? If not, do you now plan to seek them out?

15. Countless scholars and critics (not to mention the author) have observed that fairytales are by no means just for children, and that our tastes in music, art, fantasy games, books, movies, etc. are just a few ways that this can be observed. Can you think of other ways that fantasy continues to satisfy us throughout our lives?

16. Does the "Author's Note" clarify anything important for you? What did you find useful and/or interesting?

17. Rather than pure fantasy, the author chooses to place this retelling in a specific place and time. What might have been lost without the historically accurate background/setting?

About The Author

Like so many readers, writers, and scholars, Judith Rypma has been obsessed with fairytales and folklore for most of her life. "Fortunately for me, I grew up forbidden to attend movies, and so my introduction to the most popular tales was uninfluenced by the Disney Corporation's versions." Instead as a child she read tales collected by the Grimms and Charles Perrault (1697), plus original fairytales written by Hans Christian Andersen. Years later, she would not only teach folklore at Western Michigan University, but write her own poetic responses to tales. Her fairytale-influenced collection of poems, *Rapunzel's Hair,* won the All Nations Press Chapbook Award. Although this is her first novelized retelling, she hopes it is not her last!

Author's website: www.rypmabooks.com